A Village Theatre
MURDER

BOOKS BY KATIE GAYLE

JULIA BIRD MYSTERIES

An English Garden Murder

Murder in the Library

A Village Fete Murder

Murder at the Inn

A Country Wedding Murder

Murder on a Country Walk

EPIPHANY BLOOM MYSTERIES

The Kensington Kidnap

The Museum Murder

Death at the Gates

A Village Theatre MURDER

KATIE GAYLE

bookouture

Published by Bookouture in 2025

An imprint of Storyfire Ltd.
Carmelite House
50 Victoria Embankment
London EC4Y 0DZ

www.bookouture.com

The authorised representative in the EEA is Hachette Ireland
8 Castlecourt Centre
Dublin 15 D15 XTP3
Ireland
(email: info@hbgi.ie)

ISBN: 978-1-83525-868-2
eBook ISBN: 978-1-83525-867-5

*To our families, who thought we were mad when we started this,
but cheered us on nonetheless.*

'Arranging the props and accessories for the village play reminds me of playing with the dressing-up box I had as a child,' said Julia Bird, dipping her hand into the bulging bag that sat between her and Tabitha on the kitchen table. 'We had a trunk full of clothes and bits and pieces. It was my favourite pastime.'

She pulled a hooked pirate hand out of the bag and tried it on, modelling it for Tabitha. 'I didn't have one of these, sadly. I'd have loved one.'

'Very cool. Although I can't see how we can incorporate it into a 1950s murder mystery drama that takes place entirely on dry land, and features precisely zero pirates,' said Tabitha.

'We can't. A tragic waste of an excellent prop,' Julia said, tossing it back into the bag with the scarves and hats and some stranger items – a doctor's stethoscope, a crown made of plastic flowers, a fold-up walking stick.

'I loved dressing up too,' said Tabitha. She took a pair of huge Jackie O sunglasses out of the bag, examined them, and dropped them back in with a shake of her head, saying, 'Wrong era. Anyway, it's a pity we didn't know each other when we were children. We could have played at dress-up together. What was your preferred character?'

'Bossy schoolteacher.' Julia pulled a yellow pillbox hat from the bag and put it on her head.

'Are you serious? Me too! I had all the toys sitting up straight, to attention, while I lectured them on important topics. I called myself Madame Madeleine. I was French – not that I could speak French, but that didn't put me off.'

'I like to think I was strict but kind,' Julia said. 'I wanted the dolls and teddies to put their best feet, or paws, forward. To work hard and do well. For their own good.'

Tabitha smiled. 'I had literary ambitions for my pupils. I insisted that they learn the words to all the A.at A. Milne poems, Christopher Robin, and so on. I can still recite most of them, if you'd like to hear one.'

The two women laughed at the pleasure of their shared childhood experience, and in unvoiced recognition that they still both had something of the bossy schoolteacher in them. Julia had had a successful and fulfilling career in social work, from which she was now retired, and Tabitha was the librarian at the Berrywick Library. They hadn't strayed too far from their childhood personas.

The two old friends went back to the job at hand, which was finalising the props and accessories for the annual performance of the South Cotswolds Players, the region's amateur dramatics society. Tabitha had in fact written the play – 'in the style of Agatha Christie', she had told Julia, blushing slightly at comparing herself to the Queen of Crime. The final dress rehearsal was to take place on Friday, and then four more performances would take place over the coming weekend and week. Somewhat to Julia's surprise, the tickets were almost all sold out. While neither Julia nor Tabitha had any desire to be on the stage themselves, they had volunteered to help with the costumes and props, and had enjoyed themselves greatly.

'This yellow pillbox for the Dorothy character, do you think?' Julia turned her head side to side in an exaggerated way, modelling the hat for Tabitha. 'Or shall we go with the beret?'

Tabitha picked up the red beret and put it back down. 'The yellow. I know Nicky would love to wear the beret, but it's too artsy for the role. Too flamboyant. Her character, Dorothy, is a Shy Young Lass, remember, not an Artsy Parisian Chatterbox.'

They both grinned. Nicky was anything *but* a shy young lass. On the contrary, she was a contender for the title of the most talkative woman in Berrywick – an extremely broad and hotly contested field, comprising dozens of candidates.

'Okay, that's decided.' Julia took off the hat, and placed it to her right, on the 'yes' pile. She made a note in her notebook, saying the words as she wrote them. 'Dorothy. Yellow hat. Actor's own jewellery. Modest jewellery. Flat pumps.' She paused and reread the list, checking that she hadn't missed anything. 'Done. Next up, Dylan, or should I say, Julian, the Dashing Young Rogue?'

'Dylan's no more a rogue than Nicky is a shy young thing,' said Tabitha.

'That's acting for you,' said Julia. 'I saw him at one of the rehearsals, and I couldn't believe it was the same sweet young chap who wooed my Jess. Striding about, preening. It was quite unnerving to watch, actually.'

'I can imagine. Not that Jess would have fallen for the charming rogue persona. Your daughter's too sensible for that, it seems to me. How about this?' Tabitha held up a red silk scarf, spotted with pink. 'Nothing says Dashing Young Rogue like a silk cravat, I say.'

Their work was interrupted by the sudden thumping of Jake's tail against the wooden floor. Julia knew the rhythm of that tail thumping. It was nervous tail thumping. She turned to see Chaplin, the black and white cat, who had jumped in at the window next to the sink and was gazing imperiously down his nose at the dog.

'It's okay, Jakey boy,' Julia said, reaching down to give him a pat. He looked up at her gratefully, knowing she would protect him from the terrifying feline, which seemed poised to pounce from its great height at any moment and rip him limb from limb.

'How are the pets getting along?' Tabitha asked, surveying the interaction.

It was odd to have 'pets', plural. Julia had had a pet, singular, in the form of Jake, as her constant companion for a couple of years. And now there was Chaplin.

Julia sighed. 'It's been nearly three months since Chaplin came to live with us. The *cat's* fine, not in the least scared of Jake. I suppose that Jake has settled down quite a bit, but he doesn't like to walk past Chaplin in a confined space, especially if the cat is above him. He still behaves as if he is in mortal danger half the time.'

'From a cat. Who weighs about a twentieth of what he does.'

'Yes. But he's always been nervous of cats. And to be fair to Jake, Chaplin has got The Stare.'

They both looked at the cat, who had fixed its wide green eyes on the dog like lasers.

'I see what you mean, Julia. It's quite intimidating, actually. I'm feeling a bit antsy myself.'

'He's a sweet cat. It's just The Stare. And of course The Moustache.'

Tabitha snorted. The cat did in fact have a neat little black moustache on his upper lip, a perfect black rectangle which, together with his round eyes, made him a dead ringer for Charlie Chaplin – hence the name. It was a little disconcerting, until you got used to it.

'It was kind of you to take him in after Olga died.'

'I tried not to. Jake and the chickens felt like a full house. But Dr Ryan was keeping him in the vet's rooms, and he was alone at night, and if no one came forward to take him... Let's just say that Dr Ryan can be surprisingly persuasive. And I did find poor Chaplin, after all. That day...' Julia stopped. She didn't need to finish her sentence for Tabitha to know what she meant.

Julia had come across the hungry cat while calling on his owner, Olga Gilbert, the vet's missing receptionist, who was, as it turned out, no longer in the land of the living, and thus in no fit state to feed cats. 'I felt rather responsible for him. And really, he's the sweetest chap.'

Chaplin walked across the counter to his food bowl – no food bowl could be left on the floor, for obvious reasons – and began to crunch determinedly through the dry pellets. Chaplin had settled right in. In fact, he behaved as if he owned the place. Little did he know that he had narrowly escaped being shipped off to the animal rescue shelter. Jake relaxed, now that the cat was otherwise occupied.

'Right,' said Julia, consulting her notebook. 'Next up, Oscar.'

'Ah yes, Oscar, playing the Upright Husband.'

'Until he decides to get his revenge... Which brings us to...'

'The prop gun.' Tabitha plonked a small black handgun down on the table. 'Got it.'

A little shiver ran up Julia's spine. She hated the sight of a gun, even a gun designed as a prop, with the ability to make a loud bang and do little else, fit only for the stage.

'And the gun is concealed. So he needs a jacket with a large pocket to keep it in. He's wearing his own, a brown tweed.'

'Did he check that the gun fits?'

'Yes. At the last rehearsal, when Regional Superintendent Grave brought this prop gun for Oscar to use in that scene. It is a perfect fit. So, he's all sorted. We'll keep it in the little props cupboard and put it in his pocket backstage, so that he can put the jacket on and find the gun ready.'

Tabitha stretched her back and rolled her shoulders. 'Shall we take a little break?'

'Yes. I'll put the kettle on and we can go outside to stretch our legs while we wait for it to boil. Come on, Jake.'

2

Julia put the kettle on, and the two women went out of the kitchen door into the back garden. Jake followed, accelerating slightly as he passed the cat – still chomping obliviously away in his place on the counter – and exited the door in relief. Delighted to have made it outside without incident, he bounded over to the chicken coop to greet the residents, six fat chestnut-coloured hens who had bustled their way to the gate in anticipation of a snack.

'I'll let them peck around outside for a bit,' said Julia, jiggling the bolt on the gate. 'Come on, girls. Go and find those slugs!'

'Is the cat all right with the hens?'

'Yes. He watches them, but doesn't bother them. And they don't give a toss about The Stare.'

'Or The Moustache, I presume.'

'Completely unfazed by that either.'

'Hens are sensible creatures.'

Julia pulled the gate open. Henny Penny, the largest and boldest hen, came out first, at a brisk trot, heading straight for

Jake. He nudged her gently with his soft brown muzzle. She leaned into him for a long moment, then trotted on, heading for the vegetable patch where shiny garden snails could sometimes be found lurking beneath the spinach leaves. Jake followed meekly after her, his eyes soft with affection.

'Weird chap, your Jake,' Tabitha muttered with a shake of her head. 'Him and that chicken.'

'You're not wrong. But who can understand true love, really?'

'Not me, that's for sure.' Tabitha said this lightly, but Julia wondered if she didn't sometimes wish for a loving companion. Julia had thought her own romantic life had likely ended with her marriage three years ago, and no one had been more surprised than her when Dr Sean O'Connor had arrived in her life. His craggy handsome face and lively blue eyes had brought an unexpected flutter to her pulse, but it was his calm good nature and good humour that had truly won her heart.

As the chickens fanned out in search of insects, Tabitha and Julia took their own slow circuit of Julia's little garden, enjoying the soft sun that fell slanted through the trees. The leaves were starting to show a hint of yellow, and the cool air carried the promise of autumn. It wouldn't be long before Julia was raking up fallen leaves. Her mind turned to the tasks she would have to take care of ahead of the change of seasons. The garden and house were small, but somehow there was always a lot to do. She must order in more wood for the fire. Cut down the dahlias, which had been magnificent, but were now leggy and falling over. Cover some of the more tender plants. Put in her winter vegetable seeds and seedlings. Cabbages. Carrots. Perhaps she'd give potatoes a try this year.

'...don't you think?' asked Tabitha.

'Sorry. I was miles away with the potatoes. What did you say?'

Tabitha gave her a quizzical look, but clearly decided not to investigate the potato comment, instead repeating her unheard observation: 'I was saying that Roger Grave has done a rather good job of directing the play. I know you had your reservations about him, but he's been good with the actors, and quite easy-going all round. I was a bit concerned that he might not see it the way that I wrote it, but he's been really respectful of the text.'

'Yes. I expected him to be bossy and self-important, which is how he is in his professional life. But he has turned out to be cooperative and quite surprisingly pleasant.'

'Maybe his move to Edgeley has improved his mood. All that fresh air. The sheep grazing in the meadow, and so on. Calmed him down.'

'I suspect the poor man's a frustrated thespian, and is happier in the theatre than in the police station.'

'A would-be director trapped in the life of a police superin-tendent. Tragic, it is!' Tabitha uttered her analysis dramatically, hands clasped together.

Julia laughed at Tabitha's delivery. 'I suppose I'm pleased for him that he's fulfilling a life's dream of directing a play. And bringing your wonderful writing to life.'

If Julia was a little grudging in her enthusiasm, it was because she herself had brought out the worst in Roger Grave. She had had a series of run-ins with him in the past. In addition to his supercilious manner, he had taken an extremely dim view of her unofficial 'helping' on a couple of recent crime cases. Or 'interference', as he would call it. But that was a separate matter. He'd been on his best behaviour in the six weeks of rehearsal, and particularly polite to Julia. So much so that now she felt guilty for her judgemental response to Grave, and even a little sorry for him, if he was indeed a reluctant copper with a hankering for the stage. She said, in a conciliatory tone, 'The theatre does seem to make him happy and bring out the best in him. Fortunately for all concerned, we will be seeing the director side, not the regional superintendent side, of Roger this weekend.'

The whistling of the kettle called them back into the kitchen, where Julia made a pot of Earl Grey tea. She took out the last quarter of the carrot cake she had baked at the weekend.

'Oooh, I shouldn't. I've got that five pounds to lose,' said Tabitha, who had been threatening to lose five pounds since they were in their third year at university. Whether they were the same five pounds or different ones was a brain teaser that Julia could never quite crack. But same or different, she didn't think Tabitha needed to lose them then, or now. She suspected Tabitha didn't think so either, and mentioned them only out of habit. A suspicion that was reinforced by Tabitha saying, after barely a moment's hesitation, 'Ah, all right then, I can't resist that cream-cheese icing you make, Julia. But just a sliver. For the taste.'

They sorted out the last few accessories over tea and cake. There was a spotted silk cravat and a rakish fake moustache for Graham Powell, who was playing the Charming Good-for-Nothing. For Gina, playing the Friendly Barmaid, there was a frilly apron to wear with a revealingly low-cut and tight-waisted dress that she'd supplied herself. Julia suspected she'd had it specially made to show off her figure – which was indeed quite admirable – and wasn't admitting it. Tabitha offered to take a policeman's cap home and repurpose it for Guy, who would be playing the Postman.

'Good work, team,' Julia said, snapping her notebook shut.

'That was fun,' said Tabitha. 'I'll get the cap sorted in time for the dress rehearsal, and I'll see you on Saturday, for the opening. Is Sean coming?'

'Yes indeed. "Wouldn't miss it for the world," was his

response. Am-dram isn't usually his cup of tea, but he's excited to see the play that you wrote.'

'I hope he'll enjoy it. It think it really is rather well done for an amateur production.'

'That it is. I'm sure it will be a fun night out for everyone.'

3

Occasional bumps and lumps appeared in the stage curtain. Most of the audience members were far too busy greeting friends and exchanging news to pay them any attention, but Julia, already in her seat, with Sean next to her and his hand in hers, watched the bumps and lumps appear and vanish and wondered what was what – elbows and knees, bits of furniture? The chatter swelled and seemed to bounce off the high vaulted ceiling.

The hall was full to bursting. Julia waved at a few people she knew – there were a lot. She was surprised to spot Jim McEnroe in the audience, and wondered if he was perhaps going to review the show for the newspaper. But no, this appeared to be a social rather than a business visit – his new girlfriend Moira was leaning into him in an intimate way. He put his hand on her knee. He must have felt Julia's gaze because at that moment he looked up and caught her eye. He gave her a little nod and a sheepish grin in greeting.

The last few stragglers came in, craning their heads to find free seats. Julia caught sight of Tabitha amongst them. She had been backstage, doing a last check on the props. Julia hoped she'd remembered to take the gun from the cupboard, where Julia had put it that afternoon, and put it in the pocket of the coat, and the coat on a hatstand, ready for Oscar to wear. Knowing Tabitha, everything was in its place. On top of Tabitha's wild grey curls was the red beret that had been rejected as too dramatic for Nicky to wear. Unlike the Shy Young Lass, Tabitha could carry off absolutely anything, no matter how bold.

Julia stood up and waved, catching Tabitha's eye and gesturing to the empty seat next to her. Julia had saved it by plonking her handbag and jacket on it in a proprietary manner. As the hall filled up, it had been mildly awkward. People had come over looking for an empty seat, and she'd had to shoo them politely away, sometimes to head-shaking or tutting. So she was pleased when she could remove her territorial markers, and let Tabitha sit down.

Tabitha squeezed Julia's arm. 'Thanks for saving the seat; I know you hate doing it.'

'Oh, I don't mind!' Julia said, untruthfully. They both laughed.

'Hello, Sean. Gosh, isn't it full! Half of Berrywick and most of Edgeley must have come to see the play. Anyway, here we are. Warm, isn't it?'

'Certainly is. I'm overdressed in my warm jacket, that's for sure.'

Tabitha fanned herself with the programme which had been made up by Guy's daughter, who was doing Art for A levels. She'd created it on her laptop, and printed it off on Guy's small home printer.

'Is it time?'

Julia looked at her watch. Six p.m. on the dot. Hector, the prompt, slipped his head and shoulders through the curtains, frowned earnestly into the hall, and retreated. He must have reported back to the director that the village hall was full, and the audience ready for the show, because no sooner had he disappeared than Roger Grave appeared from the same spot between the curtains. It still seemed strange to see him dressed not in his sombre superintendent suit and shiny black shoes, but in slim black jeans, a dark grey polo neck pullover and thick-soled black trainers. He was tall and slim and the clothes sat well on him. His sandy hair, which was usually combed sternly into place over his head, left to right, was now gently and stylishly tousled – had it been gelled, Julia wondered?

He addressed the audience, his voice warm and confident, his face relaxed.

'Good evening, ladies and gentlemen, and welcome to the South Cotswolds Players' performance. Everyone involved – the actors, wardrobe people and other helpers – are amateurs who love theatre, as indeed am I, the play's director. They have worked very hard and put their hearts and souls into this play, *A Night to Remember*. Written by our very own Tabitha Fuller-good, and performed by a cast of talented local folk – I thank them all. I have no doubt that, as promised by the play's title, they will give you a night you won't easily forget.'

Roger took one last, satisfied look at the full hall before him, gave a small bow in acknowledgement of the enthusiastic applause, and disappeared back from whence he had come. Minutes later, the curtains opened to reveal a well-furnished sitting room. Julia recognised the props that she had arranged for the Players to borrow from Second Chances, the charity shop where she worked – a rather ugly but dramatic oil painting of a ship at sea in the sunset, a few side tables, striking red cushions on the sofa, a mantel clock, and, below it, a firescreen in front of a non-existent fire.

'Well, I must say, the stage set is rather good,' whispered Sean. 'Well done.'

When Nicky came in sporting the little yellow hat, Tabitha gave Julia a hard poke with her elbow. They exchanged glances, and shared a small rush of pride in their work. The hat was perfect. Jaunty, yet modest.

The Charming Good-for-Nothing followed her in his midnight-blue velvet jacket.

'There's Graham,' said Jane Powell, in a stage whisper from the row behind them, presumably to her neighbour. 'That's a fake moustache.'

'It's right realistic, though, isn't it?' whispered her neighbour, admiringly. 'Looks just like he grew it himself. You'd never guess.'

'He's fooling people, all right,' said Jane.

Dylan came on briefly and acquitted himself well as the Dashing Young Rogue. He had few lines, but he delivered them with panache – not too much, just enough, a pause, a little shrug. He had a certain presence about him. Julia had promised her daughter Jess a report of his performance, and she was pleased that she could give a good account. The youngsters had agreed that their holiday romance had to come to an end when Jess returned to Hong Kong, but Julia happened to know that they were in almost daily communication. The flame still burned, it seemed.

Although she'd seen bits and pieces of the play in the previous weeks, Julia hadn't watched it from beginning to end. The story carried her along quite briskly, and the acting was surprisingly good, for the most part. There was a brief flash of terror when Guy, playing the Postman, who only had four lines to say, froze on the third one. A stressful couple of moments passed while he stood rooted to the spot, gaping like a fish. Excruciatingly long moments for Guy, no doubt, but also for Julia.

Just when Julia thought she would expire from the awkwardness, there came a hiss from offstage: 'No news is good news, sir.' It was Hector speaking from the wings.

'No news is good news, sir,' echoed Guy, relief washing over his face.

Sean squeezed her hand, knowing Julia would have felt stressed in sympathy, along with Guy. 'Poor chap,' he whispered.

She squeezed back.

Tabitha leaned in to whisper in her other ear, 'Better hope nothing happens to Graham.'

Julia gave a silent snort of laughter at the wry comment. Guy was the leading man's understudy. Guy might know the lines, but it certainly didn't look as if he'd have the nerves to deliver them in a big role.

The play was a drama, but it did offer a few laughs – most of them intended, and one or two not. Within ten minutes of curtain-up, Graham's moustache had detached itself from the upper left corner of his lip and was inching its way slowly upward. Soon it was well on the diagonal. When it reached the edge of his left nostril, forty-five minutes later, it must have started to tickle, because Graham gave a huge sneeze, followed by another. The force of the sneeze further loosened the errant facial hair, which now hung down vertically over his lips, attached by a mere thread of glue, interfering with his delivery of the lines.

Subdued titters came from the audience, and a horrified whisper – 'Oh, what will people think, Graham?' – from his wife in the row behind them. Julia smiled to herself. Jane was permanently distracted by the question of what other people thought.

Unfortunately, the facial hair malfunction coincided with a particularly dramatic moment in the play. The denouement was at hand!

Oscar, playing the Upright Husband, stormed in from the wings to confront him about his treacherous lecherous behaviour.

'You cad!' he shouted, producing a gun from the pocket of his brown tweed coat.

The audience gasped. And – oddly – giggled.

Oscar stopped short, looking out at the audience in surprise. Why were they laughing at the dramatic end to the play? He looked at Graham and saw the problem immediately. The moustache was hanging comically from his face, swaying gently. Graham seemed not to know what to do about the awkward situation. He was struck dumb and motionless, blinking into the hall.

Oscar, quicker on the uptake, stepped forward, reached out his left hand and gave the moustache a sharp tug, removing it. Graham let out a small yelp. Oscar tossed the strip of facial hair into the wings and picked up where he'd left off.

'You cad,' he shouted again, waving his gun at the Charming Good-for-Nothing.

'Let me explain!'

'There's nothing you can say! You must take your punishment.'

Oscar lifted his arm, steadying it with his other hand, the pistol aimed straight at his rival's chest.

Nicky came running in, shouting, 'No!'

But it was too late for the Shy Young Lass's intervention. The dramatic tale of love and deception had only one possible end.

The Upright Husband looked down the gun at the Charming Good-for-Nothing, and pulled the trigger.

A great crack rang through the hall.

The Charming Good-for-Nothing had his comeuppance. He crumpled, thudding heavily onto the wooden boards.

Nicky screamed, a high, ear-splitting shriek.

Lights out. The stage went black. The curtains closed, muffling the sound of Nicky's screaming.

4

'Well, that was rather well done,' said Sean. 'A very dramatic ending. What an excellent story, Tabitha. I'm most impressed.'

'Heavens, Nicky could break glass with that scream,' Tabitha said with a shudder. The screaming had gone on a bit even after the house lights went up, which was rather too long for Julia's taste. It was probably one of those modern drama things, like breaking the fourth wall or whatever it was called.

'Shall we have a quick one at the Topsy Turnip before we go home?' Julia said, turning to her companions, as they gathered their coats and bags .

'I'd be up for that,' Tabitha said.

'Good idea,' said Sean, looking at his watch. 'It's early yet.'

'Attention!' came a booming voice from the stage. It was Roger Grave, standing in front of the curtains looking very – well, grave. 'Is there a doctor in the house?'

Everyone in Berrywick knew that Sean O'Connor was a doctor, and the people standing around near them turned to him expectantly. He was already on his feet, his face serious. Julia stood to let him pass. 'Coming through,' he said, briskly, pushing his way into the aisle.

'Clear the aisle! Move to the back exit,' shouted Roger from the stage. He was clearly agitated. 'Let Dr O'Connor through!'

The audience pushed and squeezed out of Sean's path, some scurrying to the rear of the hall. The few who couldn't get out of the way stood to the sides of the aisle.

'Oh, I hope this doesn't slow Graham down. He promised he'd be right out. We have things to talk about,' Jane said, as much to herself as to anyone, before fully taking on the broader issue at hand. 'I mean, I hope everyone's all right. It sounds like somebody has had a bad turn. I wonder who... Goodness, you don't think it's him, do you?'

Julia turned to address her in the row behind. Jane was short and plump, with warm brown eyes that reminded Julia rather of a woodland animal. 'It's all right, Jane. Whoever it is, it's probably just the heat.'

'Or the nerves. You know, being on stage and all,' said Tabitha. 'Or a sprained ankle, or something.'

Sean had reached the stage now and was ascending the steps.

The hall was clearing rapidly. Julia, Tabitha and Jane were some of the last left. 'I'm going to go up and find Graham,' said Jane.

'I'll come with you.' Julia rather surprised herself when she said it. She wasn't sure why she felt she had to go. Nonetheless, she took Jane's arm and the two women walked together towards the stage, Tabitha following close behind. As they approached the stage, hands yanked the stage curtains apart to admit Sean, and there was no mistaking what Julia saw in that brief moment. There was someone lying on the stage, just the midsection of his torso visible, a glimpse of a midnight-blue velvet jacket. An arm lying limp on the floor. A pale hand showing from the blue velvet sleeve. Graham.

Hands yanked the curtains shut, but it was too late. Jane had seen what Julia had seen. Jane's legs seemed to give way and Julia only just kept her upright long enough to stagger to the steps leading up to the stage and sit her down.

'Is he all right?' Jane asked Julia quietly, her brown eyes wide and glistening, her expression one of confusion. 'He must be all right. We need to go home now. Please tell Sean to get him up. He must stop this nonsense. We must be going. We need to...'

'I'll go and speak to Sean. Stay here with Tabitha.'

Tabitha sat down next to Jane and put her arm around the woman's shaking shoulders. Julia went up the steps and opened the curtains just a crack, not wanting to expose Jane to another sighting of her husband. Sean wasn't working on Graham's body. There was no CPR, no pulse-taking that would help him now. He was clearly beyond all that. A ragged hole gaped in his chest, below the spotted cravat. The front of his blue velvet jacket was purple with blood. More blood seeped from under him, spreading slowly over the floorboards.

Oscar looked as if he might be the next to expire, so pale was he. The pistol was still in his hand, hanging limply at his side. Roger Grave approached him, saying, 'I'm going to take the gun. Slowly now, don't move. Keep it pointed at the floor.' He reached out his right hand.

'What happened...? It can't... It's only a prop... It wasn't loaded. I mean, I couldn't. It...'

'All right then, steady on. I'm taking the gun.' Roger Grave moved gently, slowly, as one would when approaching a skittish and dangerous animal. His voice was low. He gently took the pistol from Oscar's hand.

Julia turned and looked back at Jane, who was waiting quietly with Tabitha, and stepped through the curtains onto the set. Sean was standing on the other side of Graham's body, a mobile phone to his ear. He caught her eye, as he spoke into the phone: '...the village hall, on Main Street. Yes... Coroner, forensics. The whole lot, I imagine. I'll tell them. Thank you.'

Sean turned to Roger. 'I've phoned the Berrywick police. I thought, under the circumstances... I explained what happened. The accident. They are going to send a detective. And a van. And forensics.'

There was a moment of stunned silence in which everyone seemed suspended in shock and disbelief.

Julia broke the silence, addressing Roger: 'Graham's wife, Jane. She's here, she was in the audience. She is waiting for news.'

'There's been an accident,' Roger said, blankly. 'A terrible accident.'

'I see. And Jane... Can you...? Someone needs to tell her.' Julia motioned to the curtain, behind which was Jane.

Roger looked about a hundred years old. His artsy outfit and boyishly tousled hair contrasted starkly with his grey, lined face. 'Right,' he said, slowly. A man who was seldom at a loss for words or self-confidence, Roger Grave seemed unsure of himself. Julia felt for him, knowing he was about to perform one of the hardest tasks there is – break the news of a loved-one's demise. 'Nobody move, nobody touch anything. I'll go and speak to her,' Roger said again, still not making any move in that direction.

'Hello?' came Jane's voice. She had mounted the steps at the side of the stage and was calling at the curtain. 'Julia, what did Sean say? What's happening?'

Roger bounded to the curtain and stopped. 'Julia, can you come with me? You know her better. It might be better if you are with me when we break the news.'

Jane and Julia did attend book club together, and although they liked each other, they weren't particular friends outside of the club. Jane was one of those people who didn't socialise much outside of her family. Julia did not want any part of giving her the news of her husband's death. She looked around hopefully, as if a more suitable candidate might appear.

'Please,' Roger said. She sighed, nodded, and took a step towards him.

He pulled the curtain apart enough for her to slip through, and then followed her, pulling the two sides of the curtain firmly closed behind him to keep Jane from seeing the grisly scene on stage.

Roger stood silent for a long minute. He swallowed hard. Jane stood with her head to the side, waiting for Roger to speak. Just as Julia had the awful thought that he was waiting for her to break the news to Graham's widow, he spoke, in a formal tone. 'Mrs Powell, I'm sorry to inform you that there's been an accident. Your husband... your husband has been shot. Dr O'Connor is...'

Jane paled. 'Shot? Where? How? Is the ambulance on the—'

Jane's question went unfinished, interrupted by the crash of the large wooden doors to the hall opening loudly, and closing hard, followed by the sound of footsteps. Detective Inspector Hayley Gibson came down the aisle between the rows of seats, with Detective Constable Walter Farmer following close behind. Julia caught sight of Tabitha at the side of the stage. Her red beret, which had looked so fun and fetching earlier that evening, looked inappropriately jolly, quite ridiculous in fact, in light of current events.

'Superintendent Grave,' Hayley said, nodding in his direction as she reached the stage. 'I believe you were on the scene. Can you brief me on the situation?'

Roger looked at Jane and back at Hayley. 'I'm afraid I can't really give you that information right now.'

Hayley Gibson straightened to her full height, which was almost a foot shorter than that of Roger. Nonetheless, she somehow gave the impression of staring the older, taller, more senior man down. 'The Berrywick police have responsibility here, as I'm sure you are aware. You are required to cooperate with the local police in this matter.'

Roger continued, 'I take your point, DI Gibson, but I must insist that we discuss the matter in a private place.'

Hayley responded in a clipped tone. 'No buts, and no insisting. I understand that you are the senior officer on the scene, but this is our jurisdiction.'

Hayley was clearly poised for a showdown. She didn't much care for Roger Grave at the best of times, and the best of times this wasn't. Julia realised what was happening. Roger didn't want to speak about the accident in front of Jane, who did not yet know that her husband was dead. Not aware that Jane was the victim's wife, Hayley assumed Roger to be pulling rank and trying to take over.

'Now. Take me to the...'

'Hayley!' Julia had to stop the DI before the word 'body' came out of her mouth. 'Perhaps a word?'

Hayley turned to Julia, scowling at the interruption. Julia widened her eyes and gave her The Look. Hayley paused, then held up her index finger to Roger. 'One moment.'

She turned towards Julia and the two women took a few steps away from the others. 'What is it?'

Julia lowered her voice. 'The body is Graham Powell. He is dead. That's his wife, Jane. She doesn't know yet. She knows there was an accident, but she doesn't know it was fatal.'

'Damn.'

'Yes.'

Hayley's sigh held all the tragedy of the world, and the weight of her chosen career path – a choice that she sounded like she might regret at this precise moment. She turned back to tell Jane the terrible news.

As it happened, this was not required. Tired of waiting, Jane stepped through the stage curtains. The high-pitched wail and the thump that followed, shaking the boards, told them that Jane had seen for herself.

5

The stage was heaving with people. The coroner's van had arrived, as had the forensic team. DI Hayley Gibson was in charge, and she'd got straight to work.

'Your attention please,' she shouted over the hubbub. 'As you know, there has been a fatal shooting accident. I need everyone connected with the production, cast and crew, on stage and backstage, to stay, please. No one can leave until Detective Constable Walter Farmer or I have spoken to you.'

There were one or two hands up already, and some murmured questions, but Hayley held her palm up to silence them. She turned to Walter: 'DC Farmer, clear the hall of everyone not connected to the production and come straight back.'

As Walter went off to shepherd the stragglers out of the door, she addressed the group again. 'DC Farmer will be coming round to take your name and contact details, and how you are connected to the play. We will be taking brief statements this evening, and some of you with more direct information will have to come into the station for more detailed discussions.'

Everyone's eyes turned to Oscar, the man who had pulled the trigger, and the one who doubtless would be first in line for extended interviews.

Oscar looked stricken. 'I don't know how it happened. It wasn't loaded. It's just a prop.' He pointed at the pistol, which had been put into an evidence bag, now firmly in DI Gibson's hand.

'He's right!' said Gina. Julia noticed that she'd thrown a shawl over her shoulders, covering the plunging neckline of the barmaid costume she'd been wearing so enthusiastically. Her hair was done up in a golden pile atop her head. 'It was just a prop gun. Roger sorted it out. Got all the right permissions.'

'It was a prop gun,' Roger confirmed. 'But I still checked it. As an officer of the law, I am always extremely careful about firearms, prop or otherwise. I'm sure you would have done the same, DI Gibson.'

'Well, maybe you didn't check well enough, because I think we can all agree that there was a bullet in there,' said Nicky, who was not one to mince her words. Or swallow them. Or even think about them too much. She was one to let them run freely out of her mouth and into the world, unchecked. 'Poor Graham, what a tragic accident. I saw something like it on this television programme, *Crime or Accident? You Decide!* I think it was called. Anyway, there was this one episode where they had exactly this happen. Only it wasn't a play, just someone showing people the gun and the bullet was in the chamber. Or was it in the... What do you call that other bit? The nozzle? No, it's not a nozzle.'

'Muzzle,' Hector prompted her helpfully, just as he did the actors on stage. He always had the right word for any occasion and was never shy to proffer it.

'Muzzle. Isn't that for dogs?'

'It is from the same root. Latin, I do believe. I looked it up once, when I was working on the television programme *Hot Press*...'

Nicky caught Julia's eye and gave a twitch of a smile. Hector had had a long early career in the popular soap. Julia hadn't seen him act. In fact she'd never watched the soap. But Hector never missed an opportunity to drop his past acting success into conversation. He and his adult son lived in the same road as Nicky, and Nicky had previously told Julia that he was remarkably adept at bringing his career into conversation, to the extent that he had once managed to slip it into a brief exchange about which day the recycling was being collected. Julia felt a bit sorry for him. An actor's lot was a precarious one, and being the prompt, and the understudy for the Postman role, must have been a bitter pill.

Hector went on, 'There was an episode with a pit bull terrier and...'

The rest of the anecdote would remain forever a mystery, because Roger Grave cut in with force. 'I'm a police officer of twenty years standing and I can assure you that there was no bullet in that prop gun!' He had turned a worrying shade of puce.

Hayley Gibson didn't look much calmer. 'That's enough. Everyone, please be quiet. Now, if you could all give your names to...'

'Maybe someone put the bullet in *after* Mr Grave checked the gun,' said Dylan. He spoke quietly, as was his way, but he had a certain presence and his words carried through the assembled cast.

There was an audible gasp, and then a pause, whereafter the group threatened to degenerate into a knot of speculation. Julia felt sorry for Hayley, who was not generally overwhelmed, but this group of amateur dramatists seemed to stretch the limits of her control.

'Oh, come on, now,' said Guy, still in his postman hat. 'It was clearly an accident.'

'Of course it was,' said Hector. 'The bullet must have been lodged in the chamber.'

'Pffft!' said Nicky. 'Accident, my foot. Prop guns don't have bullets lodged in their chambers unless someone puts them there.'

Julia couldn't help but agree with the logic of Nicky's statement.

'What do you mean?' countered Gina. 'You don't believe it was an accident?'

A babble of interjections ensued:

'How else...?'

'But what...?'

'No one would want...'

Julia was pleased that Jane wasn't there to hear the opinions and conjecture. Sean had attended calmly and kindly to Jane, and was now sitting backstage in the little dressing room with her. He'd been trying to get hold of her daughter, Hannah. Julia remembered that Hannah had had a baby not six months ago – Jane and Graham's first grandchild – and now the poor girl had lost her father. It was a terribly sad state of affairs.

'That's enough. We don't know what happened, but we are going to find out,' said Hayley Gibson firmly, keen to regain control of the motley group. Walter Farmer stood at her side, having cleared the hall and closed the doors, his notebook at the ready. 'Now. While I have you all here, can we confirm the basics of what happened tonight? Oscar, you fired the gun, is that correct?'

He nodded. His lips moved in the shape of the word 'yes', but his answer was inaudible.

'You have done that previously? At rehearsals, I presume?'

'Yes. At the dress rehearsal.'

'And where did you find the gun this evening?'

His eyes glistened with tears. He pointed.

'Tabitha?' Hayley didn't keep the surprise from her voice.

'Yes,' said Tabitha. 'It was me. Julia and I were in charge of props and accessories and such. Roger Grave sourced the prop gun, which we kept in the store cupboard backstage along with all of the other items. Julia put it there this afternoon. I took it out of the cupboard and put the gun in Oscar's jacket pocket before the show. Then I hung up the jacket, with the gun in its pocket, on the hatstand backstage.'

'All right, we need proper interviews with each of you. Let's get names and contact details, and Farmer will quickly take your fingerprints now. Tomorrow, we'll start with Oscar and Superintendent Grave at ten. Tabitha and Julia, you next. Be at the station at eleven. We will be in touch with everyone else. Make sure DC Farmer has your details, and then you're free to go. For now. I would prefer it if none of you leave the village without letting DC Farmer or me know.'

After having her fingerprints taken, Julia didn't join the queue waiting to give their details to one of the officers. The Berrywick police knew full well who she was and where to find her, and besides, she'd be on their doorstep at eleven as requested. Leaving the scrum, she went backstage. Sean and Jane were where she'd left them. Jane was on her phone, speaking quietly, her face damp with tears. She had the dull, dazed look that Julia had seen on many survivors and bereaved people in her time as a social worker. When the world has changed suddenly, permanently, and horribly, it's impossible for the brain to absorb it.

'The police said we can all leave now,' Julia said softly to Sean. 'What are we going to do about Jane? Did you get hold of Hannah?'

'Yes, eventually. Jane's on the phone with her now. Hannah had fallen asleep with the little one and her phone was off, and the poor young woman woke to multiple missed calls from her mum, and then this terrible news about her father.' He shook his head. 'Hannah was all ready to come and fetch her, but with the little baby and all, I said I'd drive Jane.'

'That's kind of you.'

'It's no trouble.'

'Do you think you could...' Julia hesitated. She had an aversion to being needy, and generally found it easier to give help and support than ask for it. 'I was thinking, perhaps, you might stay over at my house?'

He put an arm around her shoulders. 'I was thinking the same. It would be good to be together after all this shock and sadness, and tomorrow's Sunday, so I don't have anywhere to be. I'll drop Jane at Hannah's, pick up Leo from home, and come back to your place to sleep.'

'Thank you. I would like that.'

Jane turned and caught Sean's eye. 'Dr O'Connor said he will give me a lift to your house,' she said into the phone. 'There, there. I'll be there in a few minutes, love. There, there.'

6

Julia had anticipated an uneasy night of tossing and turning, haunted by the sight of Graham's body, heartbroken at Jane and Hannah's loss, troubled by the hows and whys of the terrible accident, and knocking elbows and knees with Sean with each toss and turn. Instead, she'd fallen immediately and deeply asleep, and to the best of her knowledge, hadn't moved at all.

Sean wasn't in bed when she woke up. She hoped she hadn't driven him away with her snoring. Or her sleeping with her mouth open. She still hadn't quite got used to how exposing and mildly nerve-wracking it was to take a new lover in her sixties. She and Peter had been in their twenties when they'd met, and she'd given not a moment's thought to how she looked asleep.

She found Sean in the kitchen, whisking eggs in a bowl while keeping an eye on a serious heap of bacon that was crisping in the pan on the stove. On the counter next to him was a pile of neatly sliced tomato, and another of mushrooms, as well as a smaller pile of finely chopped chives from the garden. Sean was a precise chopper, something that Julia half-jokingly put down to his medical school experience with the scalpel, but was more likely the result of his precise personality.

'Good morning,' he said. 'I'm making a slap-up breakfast, a proper Sean Special. I'm starving, aren't you?'

'Absolutely ravenous. The Sean Special is exactly what I need.'

It had been after 10 p.m. when Sean had arrived back from delivering Jane to Hannah's house, and he and Julia had both agreed that they had neither the energy nor the appetite for even a light supper. They turned in, exhausted, as soon as Jake and Leo had settled down from their ecstatic reunion.

She flicked the kettle on. 'I'll make coffee. And shall I get the toast in?'

'Yes, please. And do you think we should give the dogs their breakfast before we eat?'

'Probably a good idea, if you don't want your bacon ripped from your fingers. I'll do that while the toast cooks.'

'I'll start cooking the eggs when you get back.'

Jake and Leo were doing their very best presentation of Two Extremely Good Boys, sitting in the doorway between the kitchen and the garden, bums on the ground, tails in restrained motion sweeping across the floor like two metronomes. Only a line of drool stretching from the side of Jake's mouth gave away their extreme eagerness for a bit of bacon. The outside door was open despite the morning chill, to air out the bacon smell. Just beyond the doorway sat the glossy brown form of Henny Penny. She, too, would like to partake in the Sean Special, although presumably not the scrambled eggs.

Henny Penny was the Houdini of chickens, and perhaps the Einstein of chickens, too. She mysteriously managed to get out of the coop often – the other chickens could only get out if Julia opened the door for them and made clucking noises and sweeping arm gestures, or proffered delicious treats. Despite her very small head, Penny seemed to understand and obey the rule that chickens were not welcome in the house. She and Jake had wordlessly developed an arrangement whereby they could sit together in the doorway, but she was outside, as per the rules, and he was inside, and thus in close proximity to both the hen and the bacon. Julia knew that this idea must have been Henny Penny's brilliant solution, because – love him as she did – she recognised that Jake was certainly not strategic enough to come up with such a complex plan. Presiding over the whole scene from his place on the windowsill was Chaplin, looking snootily down his nose at the other beasts.

'Come on then, chaps. Breakfast time.'

The dogs turned and ran into the garden, narrowly avoiding Henny Penny, who had the good sense to jump out of their way in a huff of feathers. Jake sat in front of his bowl expectantly. Julia brought another bowl for Leo, and filled them both with pellets. Jake looked mildly disappointed – he'd been hoping for bacon, after all – but didn't let that get in the way of wolfing down his food.

Julia went back for the bowl of kitchen scraps, and tossed them into the coop for the chickens. There was plenty of grain left in the feeder, and water in the bowl. Last up, Chaplin, who got both pellets and pouches of soft luxury cat food, as well as fresh water. She'd rather spoiled him in an effort to make him feel welcome, and there was no going back now.

'Right, everyone sorted,' she said to Sean. 'Toast's ready. I'll put another round in for something sweet after. You can cook those eggs now, I think.'

She cleared the table and set it. She put out rich farm butter, her own home-made blackberry jam, and the honey that her beekeeper neighbour, Matthew, kindly gave her a couple of times a year. 'Half of the nectar probably comes from your flowers,' he'd said cheerily, as he'd handed over the glowing, golden jar. She got out the milk and sugar, and put the coffee plunger on the table alongside two generously sized coffee mugs. The

Sunday Times, which Sean had picked up off the mat, lay waiting for their attention.

Sean brought over the fresh tomato and grilled mushrooms, the bacon – crispy, the way they both liked it – and the pot of scrambled eggs with its scattering of chives.

'A feast!' Julia said. 'Looks great, thanks. You are an amazing breakfast-maker. Amongst your other talents, of course.'

Sean beamed. 'Dig in.'

She did just that, filling her plate, buttering her toast, making free with the pepper grinder before handing it over to him – one of the little things they shared was a liking for a lot of ground black pepper. Despite being ravenous after no dinner, they ate at a lazy Sunday-morning pace. Julia was trying not to dwell on the next activity of the day – her 11 a.m. appointment with the Berrywick police. She hoped the conversation would be short.

'I shouldn't think you'll be long with Hayley,' Sean said, as if reading her mind. 'Shall I wait for you, and we can take the dogs out for a good long walk after? It's a lovely day for it.'

'Just what I will need to blow all the horrible things out of my head,' Julia said. 'Let's go to the lake for a change. We haven't been there in a while, and the chestnut trees might already be turning.'

'Good plan. I shall peruse the comings and goings of the great and the good and the not so good in the Sunday papers while you're gone. Message me when you are on your way home and I'll harness the hounds.'

They were interrupted by the buzzing sound of a silent phone vibrating against a hard surface. 'Sorry, that's mine. I thought I had turned it off,' Sean said, standing up and reaching over to the countertop to grasp the thing. 'I'll turn it off... Oh. It's a London number. I wonder who...? Do you mind if I...?'

'Please, go ahead.'

The way Sean's brow furrowed made her sad. Julia knew

that the London number had made him jump to concerns about his eldest son. Jono lived in London, and he was absent, although not exactly estranged, from his father. He was at sea in his life, perpetually undecided on his direction, starting jobs and courses but never quite finishing anything. Sean worried terribly about him, but couldn't seem to find a way to connect with him, or help him. 'Dr O'Connor here, I missed your call... Yes, I am...'

There was a long pause, during which time Julia could hear the faint, tinny sound of agitated speaking on the other end of the phone. Sean's side of the conversation was not encouraging. 'I quite understand... I'm very sorry about that. I do apologise, and of course I'll pay for any damage...'

A shorter pause, and then Sean said, 'If I could speak to him, perhaps we could sort out...'

The agitated tinny sound seemed somewhat louder.

'I see. Thank you. Please ask him to wait there for me. I'll come. Thank you, and again I'm very...'

Whoever was on the other side must have ended the call because Sean let his hand fall, the phone hanging at his side. He looked utterly dejected, standing there by the sink. Julia got up and went to him.

'Is it Jono?' Julia asked gently. 'Is he all right?'

Sean exhaled, a long, exhausted breath. 'No,' he said. 'He's not all right.'

The relaxed Sunday-morning feel had fled, a worried melancholy in its place. The eggs congealed on their plates, the crispy bacon cold and hardening. Sean sat down. Julia sat next to him.

'That was his landlady. He hasn't paid his rent for two months.'

'Oh dear. Can you help him out?'

Sean didn't speak immediately. In spite of the closeness between the two of them, there was some reservedness around discussing each other's children. Without expressly negotiating that particular piece of marshy ground, Sean and Julia had somehow come to an agreement that delicacy should be observed in this matter. This was particularly so when it came to Jono. Julia tended not to ask questions or offer observations, but instead waited to be informed or, occasionally, consulted.

Sean cleared his throat and answered. 'I did. He messaged me that he was short and I sent him the money for his rent. It seems it didn't make its way to the landlady. She's evicting him for non-payment. Apparently he didn't pay the full rent the previous month, either.'

'I see. Do you think you can convince her to take him back?'

'I doubt it. He got upset – or "freaked out", as she put it – when she told him he had to go. Refused to leave. He went out at some point and she locked the doors. He's outside on the pavement. She called me as his emergency contact.'

'Oh, Sean, I'm sorry. What a mess.'

'It is a mess. *He's* a mess. I'm going to go and see what's going on. Perhaps I can sort things out, although it doesn't sound likely. It's not just the money. His room is an absolute tip, apparently. He doesn't take the rubbish out. She's worried about rats.'

'What will you do? Will you bring him home with you for a bit?'

Jono hadn't been to visit his father in all the time Sean and Julia had been together. First he had been studying music, and had apparently been too busy. After that, it had been one excuse after another. Sean had visited him in London on occasion, but Julia had never met him.

Sean looked at his watch. 'I'd better go. It'll take me about three hours to get there, and he's out on the street. The landlady said she won't let him in until I arrive. And I've got to go home first to drop Leo.'

'What time is it?' Julia asked, remembering her own appointment with Hayley Gibson.

'Ten past ten.'

'I'll have to go soon, too.'

He looked at her blankly.

'To the police station.'

'Of course. Sorry. I just... It slipped my mind.'

'You're worried about Jono. Why don't you finish your breakfast? Another five minutes won't make a difference, and if you don't eat you'll be ravenous by the time you get to London. And you can leave Leo here, he'll be fine with Jake while I'm out.'

'Thank you, you are right on all counts.' He looked at her, and said with a tired smile, 'As usual.' He ate efficiently, with none of the easy enjoyment they'd started out with. Sean wiped his mouth and picked up his plate.

'Leave it, I'll tidy up. Go on, Sean. Go to your son. Do what you need to do.'

'Thank you, Julia. And I hope your meeting with DI Gibson is quick and painless.'

'I'm sure it will be. Good luck. And drive carefully.'

7

Tabitha was walking to the police station when Julia drew up in her car. Julia gave a quick toot of the horn to attract her friend's attention. Tabitha stopped and waited for her to park and get out of the car. They greeted each other with a warm hug and lingered in front of the station for a moment, neither eager to go in.

'How are you feeling?' asked Julia. 'Did you manage to sleep?'

'I feel like I was awake the entire night, but it probably wasn't the *whole* night. You?'

'Like a log.'

'Goes without saying.' Tabitha smiled. In the forty-something years the women had known each other, Julia had always been an excellent sleeper, and Tabitha a reluctant one. Tabitha looked grey and tired, and her smile was tight and dissipated quickly. 'I keep thinking about Wednesday, when we were at your house sorting out the props. Do you think the prop gun was loaded then? I keep imagining, what if it had gone off? It could have been you who...'

'Or you.'

'I know. I mean, not that it's not awful that it was Graham. Or anyone, of course. And I put the gun in Oscar's pocket, Julia,' Tabitha said. 'From my hand to his pocket, to his hand. And it was his hand that pulled the trigger and ended Graham's life. I can't stop thinking about it.'

'I'm so sorry, Tabitha. It's horrible. But there's no way you could have known there was a bullet in that gun. It wasn't even a real gun.'

'I should have checked.'

'I'm the one who put the gun in the cupboard. I also didn't notice anything.'

'I just feel so responsible.'

'Well, I don't, and I'm as involved as you are. It was just a prop; we would never have thought it necessary to check for bullets. Would you even know how to check?'

'No. What do I know about guns?'

'I suppose we'd better go in,' Julia said. The dashboard clock had told her it was three minutes to eleven, which meant it must be eleven now. Julia did not like to be late. Tabitha nodded. As they reached the door, Oscar pushed it open. He almost staggered out, unsteady on his feet. His breath came in rasps, as if he was gasping for oxygen.

'Hello, Oscar,' said Julia. 'How are you feeling?'

He seemed surprised, as if he hadn't noticed them standing right there outside the door. 'Feeling? Oh, well, you know. I don't know what to say. It's awful. The accident. Graham. And poor Jane. The police. Have you seen her?'

'Hayley Gibson? No. We are on our way in.'

'Not her, Jane. I'm so worried about her. She must be in an awful state.'

'Jane is with her daughter, Hannah,' Julia said. 'Sean gave her a lift there last night. At least they are together.'

'Well, that's better than... Does she blame me, do you think? I blame myself, of course. It was madness. Amateur dramatics! The stage! And Jane. Poor Jane. The situation. What was I thinking? *Quelle horreur.*'

Julia was worried about Oscar, who was clearly (if understandably) distraught, and quite all over the place. His sentences seemed to emerge unrelated. And now in French.

'Do you have someone to fetch you, Oscar? You've been through a lot: the accident, and the interview with the police. Wouldn't it be best if you weren't alone? Is there someone we could phone?'

He didn't answer her direct questions, instead continuing his rambling. 'I was at school with Jane, you know. We were friends then. We lost touch when I went to law school, but reconnected when I came back. And now look what I've done to them.'

Tabitha put an arm around him. 'I know how you feel, Oscar. I share your feelings of culpability. I wrote the stupid play. And I was the one who put the gun in your pocket. I didn't sleep last night because of it. But neither of us is to blame. It was a prop. It was supposed to be safe.'

Tabitha's words and her acknowledgement of their shared experience seemed to calm him. 'Do you think so, really?' he asked, tentatively. 'Maybe, I mean, you could be right. But the thing is, I...'

'You can't blame yourself. It was no one's fault,' Tabitha said. It was almost as if she was convincing herself.

'Neither of you is to blame,' Julia said, firmly. 'Somebody put that bullet in the gun, and it wasn't either of you.'

The door flew open before Julia could say anything more, almost hitting Oscar as it slammed back against the wall. All three of them stepped back as Regional Superintendent Roger Grave burst out of the station, his face a tortured grimace.

'Out of the way,' he snapped. His thumb pressed down forcefully and repeatedly on his electronic car key, causing a hysterical *beep beep beep* and a concurrent *flash flash flash* of lights from a smart grey BMW parked a few spaces from Julia's little Fiat. He strode over to it, opened the door and got in, slamming the car door behind him. The BMW took off with a roar that tore the Sunday-morning quiet of the Berrywick high street.

'Someone's not happy,' said Oscar. 'He probably feels guilty too.'

'Well, he *did* source the prop gun,' said Julia. 'And he said that he checked it.'

'Yes, that. But I meant he must feel bad because he had words with Graham before the performance last night.'

'Words?' Tabitha asked.

'Yes. I suppose you would call it "creative differences".' Oscar made air quotes with his fingers around the last phrase. 'Graham was *not* happy with some of Roger's last-minute direction. And Roger was *not* happy with Graham's sudden new tweaks for the character. There was a tension between the two of them these last few weeks, to be honest. Words were had at the last rehearsal. Roger probably feels bad. I mean, we all do, don't we? Who of us is truly innocent in this blighted world? Not me, that's for sure.'

Oscar's manner was a little concerning. Julia realised she knew nothing about his life, or his family. She hoped he was going home to someone supportive and calming.

The door opened again, more gently this time, and Walter Farmer's head appeared. 'Are you coming in?' he asked. 'It's 11.05. DI Gibson is ready for you.'

'Yes, sorry. I didn't notice the time. I'm ready,' said Julia, who hated to be late, even by five minutes. 'Goodbye, Oscar. Take care of yourself. If you need a cup of tea and a chat, give me a ring.'

The two women followed Walter Farmer into the police station. They went straight through to DI Hayley Gibson's office.

'Right, hello, sit down.' Hayley was all business, barely pausing for such niceties as a greeting. 'I'm waiting on forensics; it's been fast-tracked, obviously, given the circumstances. You two were responsible for the props. I need you to take me through where the gun was at all times in the last few days.'

Julia looked at Tabitha and gave her a nod, deferring to her as the chief prop master.

'We went through all the props and accessories on Wednesday,' said Tabitha.

'Back up a bit,' said Hayley. 'When did you get the gun?'

'It must have been Monday. Roger Grave got it from a place that supplies prop guns, and he got all the licences and stood as the registered prop master for the gun.'

'What did Roger Grave say when he gave it to you? Did he say he had checked it for bullets?'

Tabitha nodded. 'He did, actually. He mentioned that, just in passing. I picked it up a bit nervously. I'm not used to guns. And he said something about it just being a chunk of metal designed to look like a gun, but not actually shoot. And then he said that there was no bullet because he'd looked in the chamber and that's what police are trained to do.'

'And did he say anything about how you should handle it? Anything like that?'

'No. He didn't have to. It was just a prop. It wasn't in use. Not for *shooting*. He just handed it over.'

'And what did you do with it?' Hayley was taking notes as Tabitha spoke.

'I put it in the props cupboard backstage, with all the other accessories.'

'Was the cupboard locked?'

'No. It's a village hall. I mean, there's no reason... I fetched all the small accessories on Wednesday to go through them a final time, and make last-minute decisions with Julia.'

By the way DI Gibson nodded, Julia understood that Tabitha's account tallied with Roger's.

'Thinking back to Wednesday. When you held the gun, did you notice any difference from when you'd held it on Monday? The weight, perhaps. Anything at all?'

Tabitha shook her head.

'Julia?'

'No. I held it briefly both times, but I couldn't say that I'd even notice if there was anything different.'

'Okay. Now, after the two of you had your Wednesday sort-through, what happened to the props?'

Tabitha answered, 'We packed them up and I took them back to the hall, where they went back in the cupboard. They were used for the dress rehearsal, and went back until Saturday night's performance.'

Hayley frowned. 'At the dress rehearsal, was the gun used?'

'Yes.'

Hayley nodded. 'Did you take out the gun on Saturday, Tabitha?'

Tabitha looked stricken at the memory of that fateful night. 'Yes. I did. I took it out and put it into the pocket of the jacket Oscar was wearing, so it was there when he needed it.'

'What was your relationship with Graham Powell like, Tabitha?' said Hayley. Hayley's voice was casual but her eyes were sharp. Julia froze. But Tabitha didn't seem at all worried by the question.

'I know his wife Jane better, she's in our book club. But Graham always seemed like a nice man. I don't think anyone would want to hurt him, Hayley.'

'Right.' Hayley was quiet, seemingly deep in thought, the pen tapping rhythmically on the pad of paper in front of her. 'So what happens now? Is it just ruled an accidental death?'

'No, Tabitha, I'm afraid not. There was a bullet in that gun, and that bullet killed a man. Someone put a bullet in it. Someone loaded that gun, and I can see no reason that they would do so if they didn't mean to kill Graham. Someone who handled the gun that day is a murderer.'

8

Tabitha made a small involuntary noise, somewhere between a moan and a sigh. She'd finally realised that she was on that list of people who might be held responsible. 'Oh God...' she said. 'Am I...? Do I...? Should I have a lawyer?'

Hayley looked at Tabitha carefully. 'Why do you think you need a lawyer?' she said.

'You just said that someone who handled the gun is a murderer.' Julia could hear the panic in Tabitha's voice. She couldn't quite believe what Hayley seemed to be implying.

'Did you load the gun, Tabitha?'

'No!'

'Did you deliberately write a play that would end with Graham Powell being shot?' Hayley's voice was calm; conversational, even.

'Roger did the casting, not me,' said Tabitha. 'You can't think that I killed someone, Hayley.'

Hayley sighed. 'No, I don't really think so, Tabitha,' she said. 'But just because you and Julia are friends of mine doesn't mean I can rule you out without following due process. It's my job.'

Hayley spoke in a reassuring tone. Tabitha nodded and took a few steady breaths.

'That means getting a fuller statement from you both, as we discussed, and likewise from Oscar. You will just tell us what you know, as fully as you can, and I hope we'll be able to discount you both as suspects.'

'What about Roger Grave?' Julia blurted out. She had had her run-ins with the man, but she didn't like the thought of him facing a charge.

'I can't discuss that with you, Julia. You know that.'

'Of course. It's just that Roger said he checked. It must have been... Well, I don't know what happened. I'm just saying that he...'

'If Roger Grave says he checked for a bullet, he checked for a bullet,' said Hayley Gibson snappily, having seemingly forgotten that not a moment ago she had said she couldn't discuss the matter with Julia. 'Now, if you don't mind, I need to take down Tabitha's official statement, and then yours, Julia.'

'Oh, yes. Of course. Tabitha, I'll wait for you outside.'

Julia sat on the uncomfortable plastic chairs in the waiting area. To avoid the unwelcoming gaze of Cherise, the desk sergeant, she took out her phone and checked for messages. Even so, she could feel the judgement emanating from Cherise. She always regarded Julia with a tinge of disapproval. She seemed to think – not without some justification, it had to be said – that Julia interfered in matters that were not her business. Police business, to be specific.

Julia was pleased to see a message from Sean, who was at a petrol station just outside London, notifying her of his safe progress. It ended with a hug emoji, a flower emoji, and three hearts, an unusually extensive selection of images. Sean was generally a single x chap. Julia stared at them, wondering what she could deduce from this. After some moments of staring, she deduced that she was a sixty-something woman in a long-standing and satisfying adult relationship, not a hapless twelve-year-old with her first flirtation, and she would give no more attention to deciphering tiny cartoon images on a phone.

She closed the message and opened Wordle, which she usually did in a pleasant, leisurely moment over her morning tea. That, of course, was when she didn't have two separate crises needing her attention at daybreak.

She got two letters in the right place on her first guess – STARE. The A in the middle, and the E at the end. It seemed like a good, solid start, but she knew from experience that it was anything but. With this configuration, it would be nothing more than chance, from here on out. There was no strategy to be employed. She would be sticking random consonants into the grid until one of them happened to be in the right place. Which is exactly what happened until she got the word FLAKE on her fifth try. She closed the app, dissatisfied, just as Tabitha emerged from the door next to the front desk.

'All okay?' Julia asked.

Her friend nodded. She looked tired, but calm. 'I can only tell her what I know. And that's what I did.'

'If you can wait for me to be done, I'll drive you home.'

'I'd like that, thank you.'

Julia's formal statement to Hayley was straightforward, and covered nothing that she hadn't already told her. Yet she felt quite exhausted when it was over, and when she walked out of Hayley's office, she saw that Tabitha looked pale.

'And thank you for waiting, Tabitha. I feel quite exhausted.'

Tabitha nodded. 'Me too. The sadness and the stress, I suppose. And low blood sugar. I failed to have breakfast, other than a cuppa.'

'Poor you, you must be weak as a kitten! You must eat something as soon as you get home.'

'I will have a nice piece of toast. There's not much else in the house. I'd planned to shop this morning. I was going to stock up for the week and drop something to Jane, poor woman. I'll go out later once I've had a rest.'

The two women climbed into the car and drove for a few minutes, before Tabitha's stomach gave an actual, audible growl. They couldn't help but laugh.

As the growl faded, a bakery appeared in the windscreen like a sign. Well, it was an actual sign that read *Kneady*, but also, a *sign* that they should stop and buy baked goods.

'Shall we?' asked Julia, already indicating her intention to turn into a parking space right outside the little shop, with its striped awning over the glass front door. 'They do a good pie.'

'These are straight out of the oven,' said the baker, coming through from the back at the sound of their arrival. She held a tray of steaming golden pies in her oven mitts. 'Lamb, pea and mint, all free-range and organic, and made by my own fair hand.'

Tabitha didn't have to resort to 'a nice piece of toast' after all. No convincing was needed once the buttery smell of hot pastry reached their nostrils. They asked for one each.

'My treat,' said Tabitha.

'If you fancy something sweet, we have a cinnamon raisin loaf today.'

It looked magnificent, its top glazed golden and shiny, studded with fruit.

'Oh, I shouldn't,' said Tabitha, sadly. 'Trying to cut back on the sweet things.'

The two women silently contemplated those pesky five pounds. 'Oh, I know,' Tabitha's voice lifted. 'I'll get that for Jane. It'll be a nice treat, and handy when she has visitors. Do you mind if we deliver it to her on the way home, Julia?'

Jane and Graham Powell's house – Jane's house now, presumably – was in a row of four golden sandstone cottages, all identical, but for the colours of their painted doors and the state of their gardens. Despite the Powells having moved to the cottage quite recently, Jane's garden more than held its own. It was small, but lush and lovingly tended, and accommodated a number of small decorative items – a ceramic birdbath already hosting a ceramic bird, a white-painted arch over which grew a climbing rose, with a ceramic hedgehog and frog peeking from the undergrowth. Julia imagined Jane and Graham drinking their morning coffee at the small, round, metal table, and surveying their pretty garden. She felt horribly sad for the new widow, who would now be drinking her coffee alone.

They had not intended to stay and visit but Jane ushered them in as soon as she opened the door. 'I'd like the company, really I would,' she said, brushing away their objections. She did seem genuinely eager for them to stay, even insistent. They followed her into a neat little kitchen, its centre table already holding a quiche and two iced cakes, and a number of bunches of flowers pushed into an ice bucket. Clearly, the Berrywick crisis cavalry had been coming over in full force.

'You can freeze it,' Tabitha said, handing over the raisin bread.

'Now, Jane,' said Julia. 'Would you like me to arrange those flowers in a vase for you?'

'I'd be so grateful. I've been meaning to do it and feeling bad about them sitting there, but somehow I just couldn't...'

'Of course not. You're grieving. Point me to the vases, and I'll get them looking nice.'

Jane found a couple of vases and a pair of scissors for Julia, then put the kettle on and pottered around with the tea things. 'How is Hannah?' asked Tabitha.

'The poor girl is devastated. She was so close to her dad. Lucky she has the baby to keep her occupied, and her husband, Ahmed, is ever so nice, and ever so helpful. A properly modern fellow. Cooks, cleans, sees to the baby. They asked me to stay the night with them but I came home. I want to be in my own space.'

'I can imagine. And if you need anything, or just a chat...' Julia said, snipping the ends off a bunch of roses.

'Thank you. I just want to know what happened. The accident, you know. I can't imagine how the gun...' She shook her head, whether in confusion or denial was unclear. 'Did you see Oscar, when you were at the police station?'

'We did, briefly. He was coming out as we went in.'

'How is he?' Jane took one teacup from the shelf. Her hands were trembling, making the cup rattle slightly against the saucer. She turned and lowered it carefully onto the table. She reached up for a second cup.

'He looked pretty shaky. He asked after you, too. He was worried about you.'

Jane nodded sadly as she put the cup down with a tiny rattle. Her movements were so slow it looked almost as if she was underwater.

'We've known each other a long time, me and Oscar. We were at school together.'

'Oh, yes, Oscar said so. That's a very long friendship,' said Tabitha. It would be over thirty years, maybe even forty, Julia thought, doing the quick maths in her head.

'It is. Very long and...' Jane stopped halfway to fetching the third cup from the shelf. She turned to Julia. 'It wasn't his fault, what happened. It was an accident. No one's to blame, I suppose.'

This was not DI Gibson's view. But it seemed Jane wasn't aware of that. Hayley must not have told her.

'Oscar must feel awful,' Jane continued. 'Especially because...'

Julia knew that pause, that significant pause that meant something difficult was coming. She knew to wait quietly, calmly, a stem in one hand and the scissors in the other. Any sudden movement could spook the speaker.

'Because he's so very fond of me,' Jane said, continuing the slow turn and the stretch of her arm towards the third cup. 'We had a real connection, from the old days, you know. At one time, he hoped... But I chose Graham. That's what it comes down to in the end, doesn't it? I loved Graham, I chose him. And at the end, we all had to live with that, whether it was the right choice or not.' Jane frowned, as if pondering the choice even now. 'And Oscar has been an enormous support to me recently. I know he'll be devastated to have caused Graham's death, even though it's not his fault. Nobody would have wanted that. I have no idea how...'

But Jane couldn't keep speaking. Her eyes clouded with tears, and the cup slipped from her hands and shattered noisily on the flagstone floor.

9

While she waited for Flo to bring her coffee, Julia wondered how Sean and Jono were getting on. Jono would probably still be asleep, if her own experience of young people was anything to go by. Ten a.m. was practically the crack of dawn as far as they were concerned. It was fairly early for the Buttered Scone, too. Julia and Jake were some of only a few customers occupying tables.

It was starting to get dark when Sean and Jono had come to fetch Leo the previous evening, on their way back from London. They had both looked shattered after hours of driving, and who knew what other stresses in between. Julia had searched for echoes of Sean's features in Jono, but concluded he must take after his mother. Slim and long-legged, with delicate features, where Sean was stockier and more rugged. Dark, where Sean was fair and freckled. He had Sean's eyes, though, she saw. Almond-shaped, and a clear, bright blue, with finely arched brows. But his eyes lacked Sean's characteristic twinkle, she noted sadly. The young man had a dull, worried air. He greeted her quietly and politely when introduced, but seemed withdrawn and uncommunicative, except when he met the dogs.

When Jake and Leo came running out to greet them, he perked up noticeably, talking warmly and calmly to them, and rubbing their ears.

'Thank you for looking after Leo,' Sean had said, giving her a quick hug. It was the hug of a friend or even an acquaintance, without noticeable pressure or warmth. It made Julia wonder what, if anything, he had told Jono of their relationship. She knew that the father and son had barely spoken in the last year or two – Jono had been mysterious, painfully elusive – so it may be that he didn't know his dad had a partner.

She'd offered them a cup of tea and a sandwich, but Sean had demurred, saying it had been a long day and there was still the unpacking to do. She saw them out. The boot of the car and most of the back seat were full with a backpack, a guitar, a box of books, some sort of electronic music desk with sliders and levers, old shopping bags overflowing with stuff, a pile of what looked like coats. Jono folded himself over and manoeuvred himself awkwardly into the passenger seat, one long leg on either side of a large djembe drum that stood in the footwell. That must have made for a fairly uncomfortable few hours from London. Julia hoped fervently he hadn't tapped out a tune as they had sped along the M40, for that would surely have sent his father completely round the bend.

With Jono safely stowed, Sean had hugged her again, more warmly this time, and got into the driver's seat. As he'd left, he had sent her a sort of meaningful look through the car window, a look that seemed to be trying to convey or explain something, but she'd had absolutely no idea what. He would no doubt phone when he had a moment, and tell her about everything that had happened in London.

'Here you are, love,' said Flo, appearing silently from behind Julia's left shoulder and interrupting her recollections. 'Here's your coffee. Breakfast is on the way. And I'll bring a little something for Mr Chocolate. Fancy a bit of bacon, Jake?'

Jake wagged his tail, and in fact his entire bottom, to convey just how much he did indeed fancy a bit of bacon. If Jake looked a bit shifty and unsure of himself, it was because he was unused to being inside the Buttered Scone. Guests with dogs had always sat outside, on the few tables on the pavement, but after consideration and consultation, Flo had decided that the Buttered Scone was now a dog-friendly eatery. There was even a sign by the door – *Dogs welcome with well-behaved owners!* – and a dog menu, which consisted of a small serving of fancy dog biscuits, which Julia never ordered because Flo always brought Jake a little treat from the kitchen, a bit of sausage or a piece of bacon.

When she returned with Julia's scrambled egg on toast, and Jake's bit of bacon, Flo had a copy of the morning paper tucked under her arm. In a frankly impressive manoeuvre she put the plate in front of Julia without dropping the paper, placed the side plate with the bacon next to it, and delivered the paper with a flourish.

'Have you seen this?' she said.

Julia leaned over to have a look.

Was it MURDER On the Boards? screamed the headline. And beneath it: *Police investigate am-dram death, as a devastated Cotswold village waits for answers.*

'No, I haven't seen it.'

'Well, it seems the police are treating it as a murder. The newspaper says that they are investigating...'

The mobile phone vibrated in Julia's pocket, interrupting Flo's conversation. As she reached for it, Flo gave a nod and cock of the head, while pointing towards the paper with her thumb. Curiously, Julia knew exactly what this obscure sign language meant: 'You take that call. Then look at the paper. Then we'll chat.'

Julia did her own little hand movement, a squiggle, indicating, 'Bill, please.'

The name on the phone screen read: *Jane*.

Just yesterday, Julia had said, 'Don't hesitate to phone if there's anything I can do,' and she'd meant it, too, but she hadn't anticipated the call coming quite so soon.

She answered quickly. 'Hello, Jane, how are you? Are you all right?'

'I've just seen the local paper.' Jane sounded old and shaken.

'I haven't read it. I've only seen the headline.'

'They are saying that maybe Graham's death wasn't an accident. They're saying it might be... it might be murder.'

Instinctively, Julia slipped into her calm, professional social worker voice. 'I'm afraid that they see it that way, Jane. It was a prop gun. Roger Grave checked that it was empty. But someone must have loaded it. The police can't see any other explanation.'

'It says in the paper that they are interviewing people!' Jane said this like it was the most aberrant behaviour that the police could possibly be indulging in.

'Yes, of course they are,' soothed Julia. 'They need to know what happened. They are speaking to everyone in the cast and crew, starting with anyone who had something to do with the gun. They've spoken to me and Tabitha. And to Roger Grave.'

'And to Oscar.'

'Yes, of course to Oscar, because he was the one who was, um, holding the gun at the time. When it fired.'

'But Oscar... It's just that...' Jane paused on the other end of the line. 'I hope you won't take what I said yesterday the wrong way. About Oscar, I mean. Oscar and me. Our old connection. Him supporting me and all that.'

'Yes, you never said what he was supporting you with?'

'Nothing!' Jane paused for a second, and then gave a small laugh. 'That's the thing. He wasn't supporting me with anything in particular. Just... You know... He's been there... Listen to me now, talking nonsense. I have been so worked up and so tired. Like yesterday, Julia, I was just rambling on. I said too much. I don't want you to take it out of context, is all I meant. I didn't know it was a murder investigation. Oscar would never do anything bad. He's the gentlest man. The gentlest.'

Jane finally stopped her rambling, ending with a strangled sob, at odds with the earlier laugh. The poor woman was really beside herself.

'It's all right Jane, it's all right.' Julia spoke in her most calming voice. 'Don't you worry about them getting the wrong idea about Oscar. I know DI Gibson well. She's smart. And thorough. She's not going to go after the wrong man. And there's the forensics, which are very sophisticated these days. She and her team will find out what happened. You rest and spend time with your family, and let's leave the investigation to the police, shall we?'

'I hope people don't start *talking* about this,' said Jane. 'Gossiping about me. And Oscar. And, well, everyone.'

Julia had to bite back a retort. Jane knew Berrywick better than Julia did, and the chances that people would not gossip were about zero to nothing. This would be the talk of the town for the foreseeable future. But Julia knew how much other people's opinions meant to Jane, so she held her tongue.

'All you can do at this point is trust the police to solve this quickly,' she said.

'Yes. Yes. You're right. The police will make sense of it all. Thank you, Julia. Thank you.'

Julia ate her scrambled egg. Unfortunately, it had cooled rather while she listened to Jane's strange declarations. Julia liked her food piping hot, as a rule. Jake had no complaints about the bacon. He'd never met a rasher he didn't like, and he snapped this one from her fingers, swallowing it in one go. Julia looked around the Buttered Scone, which was filling up. It was mostly regulars at that hour. The tourists tended to come in a little later, for lunch. She spotted Johnny Blunt, with his blue knitted cap atop his whiskery eyebrows. There was Nicky with another young mum, taking a breather while the little ones were at school. There were one or two others she recognised, and exchanged smiles and nods with. It was nice to have a regular breakfast spot, and to be a regular herself. She noted again how lucky she'd been to end up in Berrywick when her marriage had ended, and her career at the same time.

'I suppose we'd better be going,' she said to Jake. She put a twenty-pound note on the saucer with the bill. 'We can't be sitting here all day. We've got lots to do.'

It wasn't entirely true; there were bits and pieces of house and garden maintenance to do, but nothing pressing. But she got up nonetheless.

Sitting at an outside table was Pippa, the guide dog trainer in whose care Jake had been before it became apparent that he wasn't cut out for life as a service dog. He had turned out to be an excellent companion to Julia, though. A service of its own kind, in a way.

Pippa had three lovely Labrador puppies on leads sniffing around the table. The Buttered Scone may now have had a dog-friendly policy, but Pippa must have thought that bringing three puppies inside would be pushing it.

'Oh, look at them! How dear! I didn't know you had puppies again?'

'I'm a sucker for them,' said Pippa, with a rueful grin and a roll of her eyes. 'I don't know why. They are a lot of work, and after the last lot, I said I'd stop. I swore I'd never do it again.'

There was an awkward moment while they both recollected that her last lot had included Jake, and that he had been known as the Naughtiest Puppy in Berrywick and had nearly driven Pippa mad before Julia had taken him off her hands. Neither of them referred to that, but they both laughed.

'Anyway, I relented. And here they are, the darlings. I've only had them a week or so, and look how good they are.'

Jake sniffed at the puppies, his tail going like a windscreen wiper in a rainstorm.

'Ah, isn't he sweet with them?' Pippa said. 'Sit for a minute, it'll be good for them to be with another dog. Cup of tea?'

Julia refused a drink but sat down. She reached down to stroke the head and ears of the nearest puppy. It was delightfully warm and silky under her hand.

'I thought I'd go and visit poor Jane this afternoon,' said Pippa. 'Terrible business, isn't it?'

'It really is awful. I saw her yesterday; Tabitha and I dropped by with a loaf, but didn't stay. But I think she appreciated the pop-in. I'm sure she would be pleased to see you. Do you know her other than through book club?'

'We're not close, but I've known her for years. She was friends with my aunt Margaret, my mother's youngest sister. Jane was always very pretty. I would remember her better than she would remember me, from that time, of course. She and Margaret were in their final year at school and I thought they were very glam and grown-up. Margaret moved away for a long time and so they drifted apart, but I remember Jane so clearly from those days.'

'That's a strange coincidence. She told me she and Oscar were at school together too, and of course Oscar is the one who...'

'Yes, indeed,' Pippa cut in, nodding. 'Oscar's the one she went out with at high school. We all thought that they would get married until Graham came along. It was all very sudden.'

'Oh?' Julia was stunned. That was not at all how she had planned to end the sentence, although she supposed it did tally with what Jane had said the day before, about choosing Graham. She paused. 'That must have been very upsetting for Oscar.'

'He was devastated,' said Pippa, matter-of-factly.

'I see,' said Julia, slowly, trying to decide if this was important, all these years later.

'Oh, don't read anything into this. I shouldn't have said anything. It's all ancient history. And I don't mean to gossip, especially under these awful circumstances.'

Pippa looked quite shamefaced. It was true, she wasn't a gossip. There were some world champion gossips in Berrywick, and no one ever counted Pippa amongst them.

'Please forget that I said anything,' said Pippa. 'People might jump to conclusions, you know.'

'Of course,' said Julia, flapping her hand, ushering the thought away as if it were a bothersome insect. 'Out of my head already! Let's talk about something else. Tell me all about these puppies.'

10

The trouble was, despite the flapping of her hand, the thought hadn't gone away. Like a bothersome bumble bee at a summer picnic, it kept coming back, disturbing Julia's peace of mind with its buzzing, buzzing, buzzing. In her years as a social worker, Julia had learnt to pay attention to what didn't seem right. She knew to listen to her instincts. They weren't always spot-on, but they were always worth a second thought and further investigation.

She allowed the insect thought to buzz around in her brain, as she walked along the pavement through the main road of Berrywick, past the hardware shop and the butcher, past the post office and the grocery shop, with Jake loping happily at her side.

Oscar and Jane had been high school sweethearts forty years ago. That meant nothing. There was no reason to think there was any connection between their teenage relationship in the distant past and the terrible events of Saturday. In fact, it was quite unlikely. And besides, it was none of Julia's business.

But Julia also knew that people had a way of harbouring resentment. Forty years ago, Graham had won Jane and broken

Oscar's heart. Was it really a complete coincidence that Oscar was the one who had pulled the trigger, causing Graham's death? If it was, there was a certain poetic karma to it. But was it more than that?

Jake stopped to sniff at a particular spot on a hedge that looked no different from any other they'd passed. Julia wondered idly what information he got from his sniffing. Did he recognise other dogs that had been there before him? Did he smell rabbits? Maybe a fox? Did he know how long ago they'd passed by? If he did, he didn't fret about it, or make judgements or take decisions, or feel the need to intervene in any way. He just absorbed whatever information there was and moved along. No wonder he was so cheerfully untroubled by life.

Unlike her chocolate Labrador, Julia's lot in life was to be forever trying to make sense of the world – questioning, deliberating, seeing how she might make things a little better.

The question in Julia's head was whether to tell DI Hayley Gibson about the connection between the shooter and the victim's wife. Hayley didn't welcome Julia's interference in her investigations, and Julia would prefer not to have to go to her with information and look like some village gossip. Lord knows, there were more than enough of those about. In fact, it was more than likely that someone else had already told Hayley about Oscar and Jane, Julia thought, hopefully. The people of Berrywick loved a bit of a story, even if that story was older than the teller. That would mean Julia wouldn't have to tell her. She was off the hook. Problem solved.

Jake tugged sharply at his lead, pulling Julia out of her deliberations and along the road. She soon saw why. He had recognised Hayley Gibson, walking towards them as if summoned by Julia's pondering.

'Hayley! I was just thinking about you.'

'You were, were you?' Hayley said, bending down to pat Jake who could not get *over* this surprise arrival. You'd have thought she'd been raised from the dead, the way he fell upon her in delight.

Hayley's response had been more of a statement than a question that invited a reply, but Julia forged on nonetheless.

'Yes. I was thinking about the investigation, of course. Graham's death. I suppose it's on everyone's minds.'

'Not mine, right this instant. I've popped out to buy a sandwich, and was hoping to clear my head of that just for a minute.'

'It does help sometimes, doesn't it? To not think about something for a while? You sometimes get a fresh perspective, instead of going round and round on the same route. I was just thinking, though, that Oscar...'

Hayley fixed her with a serious look. 'I can't discuss this investigation with you, Julia.'

'I know, of course you can't.' Julia paused. Before she could stop herself, she added, 'It's just that I heard something. Something about Oscar. Did you know that he and Jane had a history? A romantic history? It seems that they were involved at school. Jane broke his heart, apparently. I was just wondering...'

Hayley kept her face as expressionless as the sphinx. She gave nothing away, no indication of whether what Julia was saying was news to her or not. 'Again, Julia, I'm not going to discuss the details of this case, or what I do and do not know, with you.'

'I know, Hayley, and I wouldn't expect you to. I just wanted to give you a heads-up on Oscar and Jane. Not that I think there's anything to it, necessarily. And the village grapevine being what it is, you've probably heard already in any case, so it really...'

'Julia.'

Hayley's forceful tone stopped Julia mid-sentence. Even Jake looked up nervously. He hated raised voices and any hint of conflict.

'I don't think you are hearing me, Julia. You are too close to this case. Not just close, actively involved in the crime scene! You were working with the props. Your best friend wrote the script that led to the shooting. Not to mention that you yourself handled the gun. In fact, along with Tabitha, you are theoretically one of the potential suspects in this investigation. So, hear me when I tell you that: You. Can. Not. Get. Involved.'

Julia barely heard the last few words. Her brain was stuck on the phrase 'one of the potential suspects', like a needle on an old vinyl record.

Hayley was talking again. Julia heard '...none of your usual shenanigans... And DC Farmer will be in touch to have you come in again to go over your statement.'

'Right, of course. Whatever you need, Hayley. I'll tell you whatever I know.'

Hayley's voice softened a little. 'Thank you, Julia. There's quite a list, a lot to get through, but we will talk in the next day or two. You can tell me everything you know. Now, I'd best be getting on.'

Hayley gave Jake one last pat and walked away, crossing the road, heading to the shops.

Julia was rooted to the spot, unable to move, the phrase ringing through her head:

One of the potential suspects...

One of the potential suspects...

One of the potential suspects...

11

Julia had been coaxed, guilted, and perhaps even manipulated into accepting Chaplin into the family, but on one issue she had stood firm. The cat would not sleep on her bed. She was absolutely resolute on that. She had made a mistake with Jake, occasionally allowing him onto the bed, but for reasons of comfort, hygiene and allergy avoidance, she was determined that there would be no cat on her bed. To make this clear to her new lodger, she had purchased a horrifyingly pricey cat bed, along with a cat scratch post and a cat food bowl. The cat bed lived in the sitting room, to further reinforce the point.

So, why was her neck at that improbable angle? And why was there a soft paw lodged in her ear?

Because Chaplin was stretched out, sleeping comfortably on Julia's pillow, that's why. Not just her bed, her pillow! Julia's head, which should by rights be resting comfortably on the soft-but-just-firm-enough down pillow, was positioned awkwardly between the pillow and the mattress. She opened her eyes and moved her head tenderly, so as not to stress her neck further, and gently got up.

'Come on you, that's not your place,' she said, lifting the

sleeping cat from the bed. He opened his eyes with a lazy blink, but didn't move. He just lay heavily across her hands, his legs hanging down. Jake watched nervously from his position on the floor next to the bed. He winced as the cat passed over him in Julia's arms.

'Don't worry, Jakey, I promise I'm not going to drop the cat on you,' she said. Jake got up and followed at a safe distance while Julia transported Chaplin down the passage and into the sitting room.

'You've got your own bed, kitty cat,' she said, popping him into his bed, which was shaped like an igloo and made of some sort of super-soft fluffy material that just made you want to crawl into it yourself and curl up for the remainder of the day.

Chaplin didn't feel the same enthusiasm for his bed. When she plonked him in it, he would usually sit for a minute looking mildly pained, and then stalk off to the sofa, or to a rectangle of sunlight on the carpet or, yes, to Julia's own bed. She left Chaplin in the cat bed, wondering how long he'd stay this time.

In the kitchen, she flicked on the kettle and donned the long shapeless cardigan and slip-on gardening shoes that she kept by the door. She popped a doggy treat in her pocket and picked up a bowl of kitchen scraps in her hands for the chicks. Jake shot out of the door, and sat down waiting for the treat that Julia tossed up in the air. He snapped it, swallowed it and was off round the garden, greeting the day with his usual enthusiasm. The fresh air! The smells! The grass beneath one's feet! Oh, hello, Henny Penny!

Julia massaged the crick in her neck as she watched him gambol, and thought about the day ahead. She was going to take it easy after the busy and stressful weekend. She had not a thing in the diary. She would potter in the garden, perhaps do some cooking for the week, take Jake for a walk, and treat herself to lunch at the Buttered Scone. But first, tea and her word games and a few pages of her book, all of which she planned to enjoy in bed.

She held the tea tray carefully as she walked to the bedroom and sat down on the bed, then propped it against a cushion while she swung her legs up and settled against the headboard. The gentle sense of anticipation she usually had at the thought of an hour or so of such a mild indulgence was marred by a flutter of worries. She couldn't unhear Hayley's words – 'one of the potential suspects'. As much as Julia knew that she and Tabitha were not responsible for the fatal accident with the gun, and as confident as she felt that DI Gibson would clear her, she didn't at all like the idea of being on a list of possible suspects. She thought of all those true crime shows, in which some poor fellow had sat fifteen years in prison before being cleared by DNA evidence and sent off with a: 'Sorry! My mistake!'

The second worry in her fluttering flock was the question of how Sean and Jono were doing. She had not spoken to Sean since he'd left her house with his son and Leo and a car full of clobber on Sunday evening. The atmosphere had been tired and tense, and future plans uncertain. Sean, until yesterday his own man, unencumbered by dependants, now had a troubled adult son living with him. It wouldn't be an easy transition for any of them.

Julia had sent him a message around lunchtime on Monday: *Hope all's well there and Jono settling in. Bring him for supper sometime this week. Chat soon? Xx*

His reply had been brief and uninformative.

All fine. Thanks again for having Leo. X

It was now Tuesday. No phone call. Not even a message. Julia was determined to give them their space, but even so, it was unusual for Sean to be so absent, so uncommunicative.

There was usually a 'Good morning' message, or a forwarded article, or a cartoon he thought she'd like.

'Julia Bird, you are being very silly,' she told herself in a stern voice that made Jake look up, worriedly, lest he be in some sort of trouble. She addressed herself internally for the remainder of the conversation, telling herself that Sean was just very caught up in moving Jono and his belongings into his little house and getting the young man settled. He'd be in touch when he was ready.

That settled, Julia decided to turn her attention to her word games. Before she could find her phone, it pinged from somewhere in the bedclothes. It must be Sean, she thought with relief, patting down the duvet in search of the phone. Funny how thinking about someone sometimes seemed to summon them. Her hand found the phone and freed it from the tangled bedding.

It wasn't Sean. It was a message from Roger Grave on the WhatsApp group that he'd created for the South Cotswolds Players involved in the production, cast and crew. The group was named 'SCP production notes' and the rules expressly forbade banter unrelated to arrangements, rehearsals and other matters directly related to the play.

Please come to an all-hands c&c meeting, 11 a.m., to discuss the way forward for our production after the tragic accident. RG, dir.

Julia always found it amusing that he signed off thus, even though his name appeared in the message app and besides, everyone knew he was the director of the play. She also noted his 'c&c', which referred to cast and crew. He loved all the theatre lingo, and used it with a flourish, which, again, she found amusing. But right now, she was in no mood to be amused. She was too astounded by the content of the message.

It was astonishing to her that there was any discussion to be had on the subject. Someone had *died*. On *stage*. Killed by one of the props. Surely Roger didn't think that they might proceed with the play, under the circumstances?

Clearly, she was not the only person to have had that thought, because three more *pings* arrived in quick succession.

Surely, under the circumstances, the play is over?

Discuss what???? RIP Graham Powell!!!

Ping. A third message arrived, consisting only of six crying emojis.

The show must go on!!!!

Roger replied: *This is not the forum for such a decision. Please come to the meeting. We will discuss it then.*

So much for Julia's pleasant day with nothing in the diary. Now, she had a meeting. And if the excessive punctuation and emojis was an indication, it would be one contentious meeting.

She scrolled through the messages, just in case she'd missed something from Sean. Nothing.

She picked up her phone, determined to at least enjoy her word games.

RATED, one of her handful of Wordle starter words, earned her four yellow squares. Four correct letters, each in the incorrect position. Only the R had to go.

She played with the other four in her mind, trying to think of possible solutions. The ED ending was off the table, which narrowed things down significantly.

DEATH, she typed in, and watched as the five squares turned green. 'Well knock me down with a feather,' she said to Jake. 'It's like the phone knows something, isn't it?'

Ordinarily, Julia would be delighted to get the correct answer in two goes, but the stark white capital letters in their green blocks rather gave her the shivers.

DEATH.

Jake looked up at her with a dim, friendly expression that said, 'I have no idea what you're on about, but whatever it is, I think you're fab!'

'DEATH, Jakey, I ask you,' she said, swinging her feet to the floor with a thud. 'DEATH. That's just great.'

Julia's chat with Jake about Wordle was again interrupted by her phone – this time with the insistent purr of a FaceTime call coming through. There was only one person who Face-Timed Julia, and so she swung her feet back up onto the bed, and settled down for a chat with Jess.

'Mum, Mum, Dylan's told me all about what's going on. Are you okay?'

Julia had forgotten about this aspect of her daughter's relationship with village local, Dylan. Whereas Julia might have decided to shield Jess from the drama playing out in her life, Dylan had no such reservations. She sighed. 'It's nothing for you to worry about, darling. But very upsetting, of course.'

'Mum, you always pretend to be tough, but Dylan says that you were doing the costumes for the show. That you and Tabitha both handled the gun, and that Tabitha actually was the last one to touch the gun before the shooting.' Julia saw Jess give a dramatic shiver on the small phone screen. 'Is she okay?'

'We're both very upset.' Julia paused. She really didn't want to worry Jess, but she needed to talk to someone, and Sean was so caught up with Jono.

'Hayley says that I'm on the list of suspects.' To Julia's horror, she felt her eyes fill with tears as she said this. 'I mean, I know that I'm obviously not a real suspect, darling. But it gave me such a turn to hear her say that.'

Jess leaned closer to her phone. 'Oh, Mummy, how upsetting. But you know how Hayley is. Direct to a fault. She wouldn't have thought about how it would sound to you. I bet she just means that she needs to cross you off the list, and file some paperwork about your innocence. You know how huffy she gets about paperwork.'

Julia laughed, loving that Jess knew these things about Hayley after her stay in Berrywick. 'You're right, Jess. I'm being a silly old thing, aren't I?'

'Neither old nor silly, Mum,' reassured Jess. 'But there is one way that you can get yourself right off that list, you know?'

'And what would that be?'

'Find the murderer. After all, you're quite good at that.'

Julia gave a laugh, but at the same time, she realised that Jess was right. She needed to have her eyes and ears open, ready to take any clue to Hayley. This wasn't one of those situations where she could sit back and hope for the police to do their best. This was a situation that she needed to get involved with – and clear her name.

It was as if Jess had read her mind. 'Find the murderer, Mummy, but don't annoy Hayley. That won't help you at all.'

Julia laughed. 'Got it,' she said. 'Get involved but don't annoy Hayley. No problem at all.'

They both laughed.

'Now let me say hello to that chocolate treasure!' said Jess, leaving her mother to think about her next move.

Feeling much better after her chat with Jess, Julia had felt ready to face the day. She'd had a few errands to do on the way to the cast and crew meeting – a letter to post, a pop-in at the grocer's for a few things for lunch – all of which had taken her slightly less time than she'd anticipated, which meant she arrived at the hall ten minutes early. Hector, who often saved the day with his well-timed prompt reading in rehearsals, was indeed prompt.

He was sitting on the low wall along the pavement, smoking a cigarette and drumming his heels against the stone. He looked like an actor playing the part of an actor who had been called upon to sit on the low wall along the pavement, smoke a cigarette and drum his heels against the stone. Everything Hector did had a whiff of self-consciousness about it, as if he hoped a casting director might happen by and notice him. His son was sitting on the wall some distance up the road. Hector's adult son, Troilus, was a familiar face to those involved in the show, as he popped in and out of rehearsals, bringing Hector snacks and muttering words of encouragement. Now, his long legs were stretched in front of him and he seemed to be studying his feet, a small frown on his face. Perhaps the poor chap was embarrassed by his father's posing, thought Julia, trying to imagine how Jess would feel if Julia behaved as Hector did.

Julia hated the smell of cigarette smoke, but she had resolved to herself that she was going to find out as much as she could about Graham Powell's relationships. Hector was a known gossip, so he was as good a place as any to start. She approached Hector, making sure to stay upwind of him.

'Hello, Hector. How are you?' she asked.

Hector tilted his head a little, like a man in thought, and paused a moment – perhaps for the passing casting director to fully appreciate his fine jawline – before answering, 'I'd say I was bemused, Julia. *Surprised.*'

Hector had a disconcerting habit of overemphasising certain words in an explicitly dramatic manner. It wore a little thin after a while, and Julia suspected this was why Roger hadn't given him a speaking role, despite his much-vaunted television acting experience.

'Which is not to say *unhappily*, surprised,' he continued. 'I believe it is the correct outcome. But I am *surprised.*'

Hector could be very obtuse in addition to being annoyingly pompous. But Julia played along. 'Ah, and why would that be?'

'Director Grave's missive was unexpected. I feared the production might be in jeopardy, and yet here we are!'

He flung his arms back to indicate the full scope of the gate and wall, as if it were a West End theatre with a glowing marquee above its fine oak doors, his name in foot-high capital letters.

'You think we are going to continue with the run, then?' she asked.

'The show must go on!' he said, repeating the text message from that morning which, she'd noted, he had written. 'It would be a pity not to. A *terrible* waste of all our efforts. I, personally, learnt *every line* in that play. I practised with my son for hours. Every line! I would hate for it all to be for naught. Like the time in my last year of school when I learnt the lines for all the male leads for Shakespeare's tragedies. Every word. Just to be prepared for any eventuality. Sadly, *inexplicably*, they decided to do *Waiting for Godot* instead.'

He took one last deep draw of his cigarette, holding the smoke in his lungs while he crushed the cigarette out on the back of the wall. He exhaled with an audible sigh and a thick cloud. Julia held her breath while the smoke wafted by.

Learning half of Shakespeare on the off-chance of a part sounded like lunacy, as far as Julia was concerned, but she didn't see any point in saying so.

'Well, you make a fair point. A lot of work has been put into *A Night to Remember*. But still, to continue feels a little...' She thought for the right word. 'A little callous, perhaps. To Graham's memory.' She hoped that this mention of Graham might distract Hector into a bit of Graham-related gossip. But this was not to be.

'It's the *theatre*, Julia,' he said, with the air of a wise elder schooling a naive whippersnapper in the ways of the world. 'It's a tough business. Not for babies or sentimentalists. You know, when I worked in television, on the highly rated series *Hot Press*, the lead actress had a terrible abdominal pain. It was a crucial scene. Despite her agony, she soldiered on. Brave, *brave* woman.' He paused dramatically for effect and placed his hand on his heart. 'For the good of us all.'

'Well, yes, I imagine that was very welcomed, but a stomach ache is hardly the same as...'

'She had a burst appendix!' he said, triumphantly. 'Not any old tummy ache. A burst *appendix*. She was rushed to hospital as soon as the director yelled "cut". She could have *died*.'

Julia suddenly felt very cross with the silly woman, and with the whole system that necessitated such dramatic foolishness. 'It seems to me that would have been a very silly way to go. To die unnecessarily because of a day's filming. And I still say it's hardly the same as suffering a fatal gunshot wound, on stage.'

'Take it from me. Roger is going to press ahead. He's a *true* theatre man. Like me. Takes one to know one. He won't want to close the show. He'll get it back on stage. It'll take a *bit* of a rejig, but it won't be like starting from scratch. He only has to move one or two of the actors around, and there's the matter of making sure they know the lines...'

He broke off, looking dreamily into the distance, squinting his eyes dramatically for the benefit of the mythical casting director, who was doubtless behind a tree, looking for his new leading man.

'I suppose we will find out any moment now, because here comes Roger. That's his car, if I'm not mistaken,' said Julia, watching the grey sedan reverse nimbly into a parking space. She felt quite disappointed with herself. This conversation with Hector had been pointless, and rather annoying.

'And of course this time round, there will be less friction.'

Hector nodded as he said this, as if agreeing with his own astute observation.

This was more like it. Julia put on what she thought of as her interested-and-open-to-listening face. She decided to act as if this was the first she had heard of any tensions.

'I didn't even know there was any friction. It all looked quite friendly to me.'

'On the *surface*, maybe. It was all behind the scenes. Graham was second-guessing Roger's directorial direction. Questioning his creative decisions,' Hector spoke in an undertone, his eyes on Roger Grave, walking towards them. He sniffed. 'Really, very *amateurish* behaviour. Even my Troilus thinks so.' Julia wondered why Hector's son's thoughts on this were of any relevance, but said nothing. She knew from previous experience that it was very easy to tip Hector into a soliloquy about the long-ago choosing of Troilus's name – a process fraught with Shakespearean dilemmas, it seemed – and she didn't want to risk this happening again. But Hector was in any event in full flow about the show.

'They wouldn't stand for that sort of thing on a *professional* production. Anyway, it'll be much calmer now, I do believe. Not that we would have wished this *tragic* outcome on anyone, of course.'

Hector stopped talking to jump off the wall and greet Roger Grave with a forceful, 'Good *morning*, Herr Direktor!' Heaven knew why he was addressing the man in German.

He shot out a hand to grab Roger's leather briefcase. 'Might I help you with your valise?'

Roger pulled the case towards his chest, looking quite alarmed at the approach.

Hector gave up his quest for control of the briefcase, but took up a position shoulder to shoulder with the director. Well, it would have been shoulder to shoulder, were it not for the fact that Roger's shoulder was about a foot higher than Hector's shoulder, due to the two men being on opposing sides of the height scale.

The awkward moment was relieved by the arrival of Dylan from one direction, and Gina from the other. They followed Roger across the prettily landscaped gardens to the hall. Guy, Nicky and Tabitha arrived moments later. They certainly were a prompt lot, for which Julia was grateful. There was no sign of Oscar. Julia wondered if he would even come to the meeting. She wouldn't blame him if he couldn't face coming back to the hall, and the stage. Or to the group. She'd be surprised to see him, frankly.

Roger led the group to the hall. They stopped, as if by some silent instruction, and surveyed the empty hall and the stage, across which the curtains had been drawn. The crime scene paraphernalia had been removed and the trauma scene cleaners had been in to do their grisly and necessary work. Other than a faint whiff of cleaning products, there was nothing to indicate that just days ago there had been a death on the premises. Still, it felt strange. The group fell silent. Even Hector. Tabitha caught Julia's eye and they exchanged a small sad smile, each recognising the heft of the moment, and sending a comforting glance to the other.

By unspoken agreement the group avoided the stage and gathered in the back corner of the hall, each pulling a chair from the stacked piles that had been cleared from the space after Saturday's performance. They arranged themselves in an imperfect circle. Roger took the floor. As he stood up to speak, Oscar slunk in the door. He looked about twenty years older than he had a week ago. His head sank into his slumped shoulders. He nodded to the group, who gave their welcomes in a warm, if rather subdued way.

'Sorry,' he said miserably, taking the chair next to Julia. His leg jiggled nervously up and down, up and down, poor man.

'Welcome, Oscar,' Roger said kindly. 'Thank you all for

coming. I know it's been a sad and difficult time for everyone, and for you especially, Oscar. I am very much aware that you have all lost a colleague, a fellow actor, a friend.'

They all nodded, solemnly, and there were a few muttered acknowledgements.

'Clearly, we cannot continue with this run here at the village hall.'

Nicky gave a dramatic full-body shudder and shrieked, 'Lord in heaven, I get the absolute shivers just thinking about being back on stage here again!'

Hector blurted, 'But what about...?'

'You were here, Hector!' Nicky exclaimed. 'My word, have you forgotten the sound of...'

Roger held up his hand, and they both fell quiet.

'We won't be back here. There is an amateur dramatics festival in Cheltenham in three weeks' time. The judges for the Best Regional Amateur Production will be there. In acknowledgement of our loss, and as a kindness to us as fellow dramatists, the organisers have offered us a place on the programme. My question today is whether we want to accept this generous offer, and whether we can recast and get the play ready by then. I'm not here to pressure anyone. We are a group, and we must decide together.'

It really was astonishing how different Theatre Director Grave was from Regional Superintendent Grave of the British police. The former being a big improvement on the latter, in Julia's opinion.

The cast and crew looked from one to the other, each hesitant to speak first.

'Should we go round in a circle, let everyone have a say?' Julia suggested.

Roger nodded. 'Good idea, thank you. Why don't you start, Julia?'

'Well, I must say, I was dead set against continuing with the show when I imagined it being staged here at the village hall. But it does seem different, being at another venue, for a different audience. I think I would consider it, if that was the will of the group.'

Tabitha, sitting beside her, spoke next. 'I don't like the idea at all. I don't think I would feel comfortable acting in the play, if I was one of the performers, but I'm not. So maybe it's more for the actors to say.'

'I say we do it,' said Hector, next in line. 'It's a huge opportunity, that the judges for the regional competition will be there. They don't go to everything, you know. And I don't think it would be too difficult to recast. Personally, I know all of the lines. Every character.' Hector shrugged in what Julia thought he must think was a modest manner.

'All the lines for all the players? That's helpful, I'll bear it in mind, thank you. Gina?'

'It's hard to say, isn't it? I mean, it seems a pity not to, after all our hard work, but it might be awful after' – she gave Oscar a quick involuntary glance, blushed and finished – 'what happened.'

'I don't know what to think,' said Guy, flustered. 'It seems a bit... cold. But I suppose I'd do it if that's what everyone thinks is best.'

'I still don't like it,' Nicky said, with uncharacteristic brevity.

'Even at a different venue?' asked Roger.

'Well, that would be better, I suppose.'

'But in any case, we've lost our lead actor,' said Guy.

'There will be a new lead! The show *must* go on!' said Hector, determinedly, speaking out of turn. 'It's what Graham would have wanted.'

There was a thoughtful silence as the group pondered his statement. It was a bold claim, Julia felt. Who was to say what Graham would have wanted? He'd have wanted not to be dead, that's for sure. Would he have wanted the South Cotswolds Players to be back on stage the same month, doing the same play in which he'd been killed? Hard to say.

Julia had a brainwave. 'Why don't we ask Jane how she feels about it? We'll take our lead from her.'

'That's a very good idea, Julia,' Roger said. 'We will ask Jane whether she would want the play to go on in a different iteration and venue.'

'I've got an idea!' said Hector, eagerly. 'We could dedicate the performances to Graham! That would be a *magnificent* gesture, wouldn't it?'

Roger winced slightly at the word 'magnificent', but said, 'I'll propose it to Jane when I speak to her. Now, we haven't heard from you, Oscar? What do you think?'

'I don't know if I could...'

'I completely understand.'

'I couldn't bear to have a gun. Even to see a gun after what I...'

'Heavens, no. A rubber knife, it'll be, Oscar. If we go ahead.'

'Right. But even so, I don't know...'

'Would it help to swap roles with someone else? Maybe something a little less taxing would...'

'Speaking of roles, a thought,' said Hector, who really was full of ideas today. 'Time is so short. Perhaps we should decide now who is going to be recast, so that we... they... can learn our... their... lines. Those of us who have them. If Jane says we should go ahead, we'll be a bit prepared.'

'Yes, I've been working on the new cast sheet.' Roger pulled a piece of paper from his pocket. It was the bill from the show, with a few notes in his spidery writing. He dipped his hand into his inside pocket to produce a pair of reading glasses and a smart silver pen. 'I hadn't factored in a change for Oscar – so silly of me – so let me just...'

All eyes were on the director as he scratched his head,

looked to the ceiling for inspiration, bent his head to write, scribbled something out. Sighed.

'Right,' he said, putting the pen back in his pocket. 'There we have it. So, Oscar swaps with Dylan. Dylan, can you manage the Upright Husband?'

'Gosh,' said Dylan. 'Goodness. Thank you. I'll do my best.'

'Big shoes to fill, young man. I know you won't let us down. And Oscar, you can take Dylan's role as Interfering Neighbour. No guns involved; in fact, no weapons of any kind. All right?'

Oscar nodded, 'No guns, no guns.'

'Guy is the understudy for the lead, so he will step into the breach and take Graham's role of the Charming Good-for-Nothing.'

This came as quite a surprise, given Guy's freeze on the first night. Guy clearly thought so too, because he looked up in astonishment, or perhaps terror.

'I just wanted to mention...' Hector said. Roger looked up from his notes. 'That I know all the lines. I have the memory for it.' He tapped his head. 'All in here.'

'Excellent, that's very helpful. Thank you for reminding me, Hector. Yes indeed. Let me see where I can put you.' Roger looked back down at his notes. 'I'd like you to take over Guy's role, if you can?'

'The Postman?' Hector said, incredulous. 'You want me to play the Postman?'

'It's short notice, I know, but we all have to do our bit, Hector. I'll take over as prompt for the performances. You'll be fine.'

'Could I have a word?' Hector said, dropping his voice to a stage whisper. 'In private.'

'In a moment. First...'

'I can't be back here. I can't be in the play – I'm a murderer!' Oscar said loudly. 'I killed a man. I pulled the trigger and shot a man.'

'Oh, Oscar,' said Julia, placing a calming hand on his shoulder. She could feel his body shaking uncontrollably. 'It was not your fault, it was an accident.' She might have had her suspicions about Oscar, but seeing how distressed he was, she felt sure now that this was no cold-blooded murderer.

'You heard what the police said: there's no such thing as an accident...' He gulped for breath. 'I know that. I'm a lawyer, aren't I? Family law, but still. Anyway, I'll be disbarred. And rightly so! I discharged the weapon. The man that pulls the trigger is the murderer, that's what the law says. I know the law. I shot the gun.'

Oscar made a horrible rough gasping sound. He was in a full-blown panic attack, or perhaps even a more serious breakdown.

Julia thought about what to do. Oscar was becoming hysterical. 'Shall we take a little walk and get some air, Oscar? It might clear your head, calm you down.'

'Don't you see, Julia? I don't deserve to be calm. I killed Graham Powell and I will take the punishment. There was a time I wished him dead and now he *is* dead. At my hand, don't you see? I am going to turn myself in. It's the only way. I must be punished. It's the only road to redemption. The law requires redemption.'

Every member of the group had their eyes fixed on the rambling, raving man, and with the exception of Julia, they appeared to be struck dumb.

Oscar jumped to his feet, his eyes glittering. 'I must see that detective at once. I pulled the trigger. I pulled the trigger... She must know me for what I am... I shot the gun...'

He started towards the door muttering, 'Air... I need air... And the police... I'm going to the police...'

Julia didn't know what to do, but she knew she couldn't let him leave alone in that state. She stood up. 'Well, if you insist on turning yourself in, Oscar, I'll keep you company.'

12

Oscar had calmed down from the height of his panic attack, but his anxious pacing across the police station waiting area and his occasional low muttering was driving Julia a bit mad. Cherise, the desk officer, had phoned DI Hayley Gibson, who was apparently close by.

'She asks that you wait for her. She won't be more than a few minutes,' said Cherise pleasantly, as if it was the most ordinary thing in the world to have a man, who had just a few days before been brought in for questioning and sent on his way, arrive at the station pacing and muttering and demanding to be arrested for murder.

And here they were, waiting. Oscar, Julia, and a young woman in a rust-coloured hijab, rolling a sweet little boy in a pushchair back and forth, back and forth, his eyelids almost closing, and then fluttering open. Julia had overheard the woman telling Cherise that she had heard a scraping noise and come out of the hardware shop to find a deep scratch running the length of her car. Whoever had hit the car had driven off, but she could see from the paint scratch left behind that it was a red car. 'Bloody tourists,' Cherise had muttered, listening to the story.

Julia envied the young mum her comparatively small and manageable problem, although it doubtless felt overwhelming and stressful to her.

Julia sighed quietly at the loss of her own imagined day of applying her mind to the vexed question of who on earth could have wanted Graham dead. You would imagine that sitting in a police station with a man who wanted to turn himself in for the crime would have solved the issue, but it very much didn't. If anything, Oscar's episode was making it clear that he was the least likely suspect.

Instead of hunting down clues, she found herself in an uncomfortable moulded plastic chair in the police station, surveying the informative posters and announcements on the noticeboard, in the company of the one person that she was almost sure was *not* the murderer. Given her surprisingly regular visits to the station, Julia had already read all of the posters multiple times, and internalised their messages: *Don't fall for Internet scammers!* and *Be Fire Aware!* and *We're recruiting! Join Cotswold Police in serving your community* and *Phone numbers you should know.* She sighed again.

You volunteered to come, she told herself sternly, *and quite rightly. The man needs your help.*

But not from the police. What he needed was medical or psychological attention. Julia had an idea. She got up and said quietly to Oscar, 'Going for a breath of fresh air. I'll be right outside the door.'

Oscar nodded in a disinterested sort of way, and walked back in the direction of the noticeboard.

Once outside, Julia phoned Sean. It was a long shot – if she was lucky, she would catch him between patients, or on his mid-afternoon tea break. She was in luck.

'Julia, hi. I was going to call you this afternoon. I'm sorry. It's just been so frantic with Jono and I meant to...'

She cut his flustered apology short. 'That's fine. No need for an apology. I need a bit of advice.' She explained the situation in two or three quick sentences.

'Oscar is a patient of mine,' Sean said, a little reluctantly. Julia supposed that, strictly speaking, even admitting that was a breach of patient–doctor privilege. 'If he's prepared to come and see me, I'll fit him in today. Perhaps a chat and a mild anti-anxiety medication might help.'

'Thank you.'

'Julia,' he said quickly, as she made to end the call. 'Would you like to have supper tonight? With me and Jono?'

She hesitated only a moment, before saying, 'Thank you, that sounds lovely.' Feeling like she had achieved something, she went back into the station.

Hayley Gibson walked through the glass doors at a rapid clip. Her clever eyes surveyed the scene – the young woman with the baby, Oscar's pacing, Julia's air of mild irritation mingled with concern.

'Hello, Oscar.'

Oscar stilled for a moment, and his face softened in relief at the sight of her. He started to talk, a little less manically. 'Good, there you are. The murderer is the person who pulls the trigger. I understand this now. I'm a lawyer, as you know. And I pronounce myself guilty. I'm the murderer, you see.'

The young woman overheard his confession and pulled the pushchair closer. She leaned protectively over her child, her wide eyes fixed on the raving murderer a few steps away.

'Let's talk in my office,' Hayley said quickly. 'We can sort things out there.'

'I pulled—'

'Come on, Oscar,' Julia said, cutting off his exclamation, and ushering him towards the door that led to the offices behind.

Hayley gave the young woman a reassuring smile and led the way into her office, which was the usual fire hazard of piles of paper, but with the addition of a waxy white orchid in a blue ceramic pot, placed in a little clearing at the edge of the desk. It was so startling in its brilliant white beauty that Julia stopped and stared.

'A gift,' said Hayley, brusquely. She motioned for them to sit.

'Lovely,' said Julia, and it was, although somehow its pristine presence made the rest of the place look worse.

'I pulled the trigger,' Oscar said loudly, bringing everyone back to the matter of the day. His brief period of calm had ended, and he was agitated, his leg jumping up and down.

'Yes, Oscar. I know you did. We talked about it when you gave me your statement, remember?' Hayley spoke calmly, and clearly. It was the sort of voice a professional used when conversing with someone not quite in control of their faculties. Julia recognised it, having used it many times herself.

'Oscar, is there any new information that you have that can help us understand what happened to Graham?' Hayley asked.

Oscar peered deeply into the detective's face and spoke to her slowly, and with emphasis, as if she was not very bright: 'Yes. New information. The *murderer* is the person who discharges the weapon. I shot the gun. Criminal law 101. So *I'm* the murderer.'

'Yes, Oscar. We know you did. But did you know there was a bullet in the gun?'

'Of course I did not! I am not a cold-blooded killer. But I am a *murderer*. Now you must arrest me!'

Hayley caught Julia's eye, and an unspoken moment passed between them, acknowledging Oscar's state.

Julia spoke. 'Oscar, you've been through terrible stress. Dr O'Connor was just on the phone. He wondered if you might come and see him for a chat. It might help to talk.'

'Oh,' Oscar said. 'Oh yes, Dr Sean... A chat...'

He seemed to be considering the offer.

'But what about the police?' he asked, looking over at Hayley. 'My arrest cannot be delayed... I should stay here.'

'You go and see Dr Sean,' Hayley said quickly. 'You can always come back later if necessary. And I know where to find you if I need more information from you in the meantime.'

'That's a good idea,' Julia said encouragingly.

'Well, if the detective thinks it's best, I'll go,' said Oscar. 'But you must make a note on your papers. I am the murderer.'

'Come on then,' said Julia, silently waving goodbye to the possibility of even the smallest bit of pottering. 'I'll give you a lift.'

After dropping Oscar at Sean's rooms, and handing him over to Sean's kindly receptionist, Julia's day had been much smoother, although empty of any ideas as to how she could clear her name. She was most pleased when evening fell, and it was time to visit Sean for supper. Over the cacophony of delighted barking on either side of the front door, Julia heard Sean call out, 'Could you let Julia in, Jono? My hands are dirty.'

A long minute later, the door opened and Jono appeared, his hair shaggy and lopsided, as if he'd been roused from sleep. 'Oh, hi,' he said. He stood there for a minute blinking, and then seemed to remember how doors work, and stepped aside to let her in. The dogs, meanwhile, were greeting each other enthusiastically, with little yelps of pleasure and a blur of noses and tails. 'Steady on, Leo,' Jono said quietly, reaching a hand down to rest on the dog's head. Leo stopped in his tracks, leaning against the young man's leg.

Jake seemed to pick up on the vibe, and came to a halt. The two dogs trotted calmly after Julia and Jono into the kitchen, where Sean was grating a block of cheese onto a wooden board. He put the cheese down, wiped his hands on his apron, and gave her a hug. It was quick but firm, and when he released her, she sensed that he would have liked to linger. That he had missed her, as she had missed him these last few days. Jono leaned awkwardly at the door frame, Leo at his feet.

'For the cauliflower cheese,' Sean said, indicating the pile of yellow curls. 'The chicken's in the oven. It'll be half an hour still.'

'You have been busy! A full day in the rooms, and such a good supper.'

'Ah well, I've got my lad home.' Sean turned to Jono with a broad smile. 'And the weather's turning chilly, so I thought I'd make something hearty. And there'll be leftovers for a while. We can't be having frozen pizzas like a couple of saddos, hey, Jono?' His voice was cheery, but in an unfamiliar way that seemed a little forced, as if he was trying too hard. Hardly surprising, given that father and son had spent so little time together in the past few years.

'Yeah. Thanks, Dad.'

Sean poured Julia a glass of Merlot, and one for himself. He glanced up at Jono, and back at the wine, and hesitated before putting the cork back in the bottle, hitting it firmly twice with the flat of his hand. It was a moment that seemed to have some heft to it, some unspoken significance.

'Would you set the table, Jono? The cutlery is in the drawer in the sideboard. '

'Sure.' Jono patted his thigh once as he exited, and the two dogs followed him, walking calmly at his heel.

With Jono out of the kitchen, Sean seemed to release a little of the tension he had been carrying in his body. Julia didn't remark on this – it was none of her business and now wasn't the time – but asked, simply, 'How was your day?'

'Busy!' He smiled. 'A full day of patients, and then Oscar.'

'It was kind of you to offer to see him at such short notice. Thank you.'

He smiled and waved her thanks away, saying, 'He is calmer. We had a good talk, and I gave him some medical advice.' Julia took this to mean a prescription, but of course Sean wouldn't say. 'I sent him home in a taxi. He assured me he had someone to be with for the evening.'

'As far as I know, he doesn't have a partner, but I hope he's got a good friend. He's dealing with a lot of guilt.'

'It wasn't his fault, but still, it's an awful situation.'

'I'm sure he appreciated your help. And now, after all that, you're making a slap-up dinner. You're a good man.'

'Well, I try. Not always successfully,' he said. He sighed, and went back to practical matters. He spoke quietly, knowing Jono was in the next room. 'I'd forgotten how much young men eat. I made us a couple of sausages and some green beans yesterday and when we'd finished – which took all of about four minutes – the poor chap had to have three slices of toast and peanut butter to fill up.'

'Hollow legs, my dad used to call it.'

'Yes. Hence the chicken. I want him to feel at home, and comfortable. And not hungry!' Sean took her hand and held it firmly. 'I'm sorry I've been so absent. There's been a lot to do, getting Jono settled. Quite an adjustment. He's very... lost. And sad, I think. Quiet. I don't know quite what to do with him.'

'I understand. It looks like you are making a good start. Remember, you're not alone. I'm here if you want to talk. Or bring him over for supper.'

'I know. And there's a lot I want to talk to you about when we have the time and the space. Supper would be good, too. I've told Jono about us, by the way.'

'About us? Oh dear,' she teased. 'What did you say, exactly?'

Sean didn't adopt her joking tone, but looked into her eyes and said seriously, 'I told him that I'd met a warm and clever and beautiful woman, and that we are in a relationship, and that it makes me very happy.'

Julia flushed, and stammered, rather inelegantly, 'Likewise, Doctor.'

He leaned in and kissed her softly. 'Come on. Let's go through.'

They took their wine into the sitting room, where Jono was sitting on the carpet. He had a guitar in his hands and was picking a gentle melody, something that sounded jazzy and bluesy and a little mournful, but in a lovely way. Leo's golden head rested on one of his knees. Jake was tucked in next to him on the other side looking blissful, as if transported by the music. Jake had not hitherto shown any sign of being a music aficionado, so Julia assumed it was Jono's presence or the warmth of his leg that was transporting him.

Jono stopped playing when he saw his father and Julia appear.

'That's beautiful,' said Julia. 'What is it?'

'"The Wedding", by a South African composer, Abdullah Ibrahim.'

'Ah, I didn't realise you were a jazz man,' she said. 'For some reason I imagined you played, more, like... pop music.' She felt about a hundred and four years old saying this, knowing that these were probably not only the wrong words, but out of date by thirty years.

'My band is more post-punk garage rock, with a kind of alt feel, but I play jazz too, when I'm on my own.'

As she'd suspected, she had only the very vaguest idea what that meant, but it was about the longest sentence she'd heard Jono utter, which she took as progress.

'It's lovely to have music in the house. And I see the dogs like it too.'

'That's not the music, that's Jono,' said Sean proudly. 'Ever since he was little, animals have loved him. Stray dogs would follow him home; cats would choose his lap to sit on.'

Jono rested his guitar on his knees and stroked a dog with each hand. 'I like animals and they like me.'

Julia smiled. One of the things that she had noticed when she was a social worker was that the troubled young men who had a connection with an animal – a family pet or a stray that they had taken in or a neighbour's friendly dog – seemed to have a better chance of a happy outcome. It wasn't a scientific observation by any means, and Julia was sure that many people would disagree with her. But she believed it. Jono was the type of lad who was going to be okay. Berrywick would work its magic on him.

13

In retrospect, Julia thought it had been a mistake to continue with the play. They should have called it quits when Graham died. They should have thanked the am-dram festival organisers for their offer of inclusion, and declined. But all that 'show must go on' nonsense of Hector's had gone to their heads. And now they'd been summoned by Roger to another emergency meeting.

She had muttered as much to Tabitha, who seemed more accepting of the state of affairs, but there was no time to discuss it, because it was 3 p.m. on the dot and Roger was taking the floor. He stood and raised his hand.

'Fellow thespians!' he said, thespianly, by way of greeting. 'I come to you with good news, difficult news, and a conundrum.'

Julia was torn between wishing she hadn't come, intrigue as to the nature of the news, news and conundrum, and the hope that something might tip her off as to who might have had a murderous grudge against Graham Powell.

'Jane has given us her blessing to stage the production at the festival. If we wish to go ahead, she has no objection.'

There was some appreciative muttering.

'In the more difficult news, Oscar phoned me yesterday afternoon to tell me that after much thought and discussion, he has decided not to return to our group for this production.'

Understanding nodding and murmuring greeted this announcement. Julia wondered who Oscar had discussed it with. Jane?

'Which brings us to our conundrum. We need to rearrange our cast once more. I will need someone to fill Oscar's shoes. It's a speaking role, so...'

'Let me do it!' Hector said, jumping to his feet. For unexplained reasons, Hector had, as usual, brought his son Troilus with him to this meeting. Troilus had seemed to be nodding off and looked most startled by Hector's sudden burst of energy.

'Well, that's a very generous offer...' Roger looked awkward, even shifty.

'I know *all* the lines, every single one.' Hector spoke passionately, using theatrical arm movements to reinforce his point. 'Don't I, Troilus?'

Troilus nodded vigorously, 'That you do, Papa, that you do.' Julia could only imagine the hours that the poor young man had spent listening to his father orate.

'And as you know – I have *extensive* experience in front of the camera. I may not have mentioned, but I had a major role on *Hot Press*.'

Roger looked like a man caught in a conundrum worse than the conundrum he'd been previously caught in.

'Allow me to *demonstrate* to you...' Hector said. He cleared his throat, and looked at Roger expectantly.

'Ah, well, that's a nice offer, but not necessary. I do believe you when you say you know...'

'I insist! It's only right that I have the chance to audition.' Hector stood, feet apart, head held high. He was an actor at the ready.

Julia got the distinct impression that Roger didn't want to

hear Hector's demonstration. But he must have realised he had no choice, because he sighed in what seemed like resignation, and said, 'Go ahead then, Hector.'

Hector nodded. 'I'll take it from where Charming Good-for-Nothing first makes his intentions known.'

Ah, so Hector was going for broke. Despite the fact that the lead was not up for grabs, Hector seemed to be auditioning for it! Audacious, thought Julia. Audacious audition action from the ambitious prompt! Well, good luck to him.

Hector cleared his throat once more, and spoke in a clear, forceful voice.

'My dear *young* lady, please, allow me *to* be of assistance. As a man with some experience in the *ways* of the human heart, I *have* no motive than to assist you in *navigating* the affairs of *your* heart. I, myself, have some experience *in* this field, and am much *acquainted* with the minds of men – men like your betrothed – and can *plainly* see...'

Julia cringed. Hector's acting was terrible, just *terrible*! That's why Roger hadn't given him a bigger role from the beginning. He must have heard him bludgeoning his way through his lines before. And now here was Hector, re-auditioning. It was utterly excruciating. Julia could hardly watch. In fact, she had taken to examining her hands, which were clasped in her lap, writhing in horror, while Hector plodded his way through the lines. He wasn't inaccurate in his claim that he knew every single word, or so it seemed from his performance so far. But the way he put them together... Lord above, it was as if each word existed in a completely separate universe from its neighbour, and they were individually plodding along one after the next after the next until one decided – randomly, and without warning or logic – to burst forth with *emphasis*, calling undue attention to itself for no reason whatsoever. The one thing she must not do was to look at Tabitha, or, in fact, she must not think about Tabitha at all. Since childhood, she had been horribly susceptible to being set off by other people's illicit, barely controlled laughter. From the moment she and Tabitha had become friends, at university, their shared ability to get the giggles together had landed them in trouble. And once they started...

Which is why when Julia glanced up, momentarily, she did so explicitly *not* in the direction of Tabitha. The faces before her were frozen in awkward expressions that indicated either embarrassment, or a desperate wish to be elsewhere. Gina was staring at the ceiling. Dylan was staring at the floor. Only Troilus was looking at his father in rapt attention. Nicky, unfortunately, happened to be looking in Julia's direction, and Julia accidentally caught Nicky's eye. Caught Nicky's whole face, actually, which was in the process of performing a remarkable dance, flitting from amusement to horror to confusion to: *Oh my God, please don't let me laugh*.

Julia felt her own laughter rising, and quickly looked down at her hands again. She was a woman over sixty, which meant that the sight of the backs of her hands was guaranteed to wipe the smile off her face. Good heavens, if the skin wasn't exactly like that of the Galápagos tortoise she'd seen on the Nature Channel, the oldest living animal in the world, encased in deep, dusty-grey wrinkles. It was the gardening that did it. That and the washing-up. No matter how regularly she rubbed in the hand cream, they still looked ancient. The laugh was now thankfully under control.

But then she heard Nicky cough, a cough that Julia felt sure was covering an emerging bubble of laughter. This wasn't good. Julia could feel her own bubble struggling to emerge. The important thing was not to look up. Julia pulled herself together, staring fixedly at her hands, thinking resolutely of ageing tortoises, and breathing evenly.

Hector was still at it: 'We are alike, *you* and I. In your heart beats *a* fire yet *un*fulfilled...'

'Thank you, Hector,' Roger said, cutting him off, to the relief of all. 'I think I've seen enough.'

Troilus clapped energetically. 'Bravo, Papa. Encore.'

Definitely *not* an encore, hoped Julia.

'I mean to say, I have what I need to make some decisions about the casting, and get back to you all, if you don't mind.' Roger looked drained by the morning's activities, not to mention the previous days' events, and the prospect of rejigging the cast list again, and – presumably – disappointing Hector. There was absolutely no way he could give the man more than three or four consecutive words to say.

'Thank you, everyone. I'm sorry to take up more of your time, but hopefully we'll be ready to rehearse with the new cast shortly.' The group was already on the move, picking up hand-bags, scraping chairs across the floor. Roger spoke above the noise: 'Could the props people stay behind, please? I just want to make sure everything is good to go once we've sorted out the roles.'

Roger Grave looked a bit more relaxed once the cast had left, and it was just him, Tabitha and Julia in the village hall. He exhaled audibly, and said, 'Goodness, who would have thought amateur dramatics would be so... fraught?'

'Not me, that's for sure,' said Tabitha. 'But don't worry about the props. It should all be there except for what, um, Graham was wearing. The police have those. We'll sort out wardrobe for Graham's replacement. It shouldn't be too much trouble.'

'And we'll need a substitution for Oscar's jacket, too,' said Julia. 'I think the police still have that. If we're lucky, whoever plays that role will have something suitable.'

'Let's go and check what's what.' Roger led the way back-stage, to the props cupboard. It was strange being back there. So much had changed since Julia and Tabitha had done the pre-dress performance check. Julia could still see it in her mind's eye, the gun, lying in the props box. She'd held it, and not enjoyed the feeling – the heft of it, the hard metallic chill, had felt dangerous, even ominous. She'd told herself she was being silly, it wasn't loaded, it was just a harmless lump of metal. But look what had happened.

'Shall we get started?' Tabitha said, breaking Julia's reverie.

'Of course.' Julia pulled out the box of props. The clothes were hung on hangers on a rail next to the cupboard. There were two or three empty hangers, where Graham's costume and Oscar's jacket had hung.

Roger had the wardrobe list and the props list, and they went through them. It was all there, except for Oscar's jacket, everything Graham had been wearing, and, of course, the gun.

Julia started packing things back in the box. The sunglasses, the yellow pillbox hat, the hairy caterpillar of a fake moustache.

'Graham's moustache!' Tabitha said, holding the thing rather distastefully. 'Odd that that's here. Graham was wearing it on the night, remember?'

'How could I forget?' said Roger, with a shudder. 'It had come unstuck and was making its way down his face.'

Tabitha looked at the moustache with a thoughtful frown. 'I would have thought the police would have it.'

'I expect that they do. But remember, Graham was wearing the cheap replacement that we found. That's the one the police will have,' said Julia. 'Turned out Graham left the original at home after the dress rehearsal. Jane found it. She brought it over that afternoon and put it in the props cupboard. She told me it was there, but it slipped my mind. In fact, we laughed about it – her finding the horrible thing on his bedside table.'

'You're right. That's what happened,' said Tabitha. 'Jane put this one back in the props cupboard on Saturday afternoon, and Graham must have picked up the cheap stick-on one we'd found as back-up. That's why the moustache slipped on the night.'

'Oh God,' said Roger. 'Remember how ridiculous it looked. To think that I thought that *that* was going to be the worst thing that went wrong that night.' He looked quite distressed, but before Julia could say anything to comfort him, his phone rang. He glanced at it. 'Hayley Gibson,' he said. 'I better take it, she promised to let me know when the forensics came back.'

He answered the call, and took some steps away from Julia and Tabitha, as if this would prevent them hearing his rather loud, carrying voice. After greeting Hayley, he made some grunting noises of agreement, and then said, 'Strange. Oscar's and mine and Tabitha's you say. But not Julia's. Interesting.'

He took another step away from the two women, and carried on speaking, "Uh huh... yes, quite... indeed... thank you.'

He ended the call and turned to find Tabitha and Julia staring at him.

'That was about the gun,' Julia said, after a pause. 'It had your fingerprints, Tabitha. And Oscar's.'

'You weren't really supposed to hear that,' said Roger, blushing.

'You've got a voice like a foghorn, Roger,' said Tabitha.

'That's not true,' said Roger. Loudly.

But Julia carried on thinking aloud, undistracted. 'But I also handled the gun that day. I put it in the cupboard. My prints should have been on it, too.'

The three of them looked at each other, each coming to the same conclusion. But it was Julia who voiced it.

'Whoever put the bullet in the gun did so after I put it in the cupboard, and they wiped it clean. Whoever murdered Graham put the bullet in the gun after I put it in the props cupboard, but before you took it out. Isn't that right, Roger?'

The three of them all looked at each other. This put an entirely new spin on things.

14

It was the most peaceful walk Julia had ever had since she had adopted Jake. The Guide Dog School dropout had been the terror of Berrywick and surrounds. Chasing geese, stealing ice creams and biscuits from small children, threatening to topple the elderly. Rolling in lord knew what.

He'd calmed down in the three years she'd had him, that was for sure, but he was still a ball of energy. Unpredictable energy. On a walk like this, he'd usually be tearing about the place.

But look at him now, trotting calmly alongside Jono, with Leo on his other side, their tails wagging in tandem, like a cheerful metronome. The dogs weren't even on leads, but they stayed on the path, on Jono's left, keeping pace with his brisk walk. Jono stopped at the junction between the path and the cross path. He made a small hand gesture, and the dogs stopped too. They looked at him, calm but alert, awaiting instruction.

'It's like he can control them with his mind,' Julia whispered.

Sean shook his head in wonder. 'It's amazing. But it's like the dogs have some weird effect on him too. They calm him.'

From her position some feet behind Jono and the dogs, Julia saw another dog approaching. It was a very large dog in a harness, the lead held lightly in the hand of a young woman wearing a bright yellow polo neck under baggy denim dungarees. There was something odd about the animal's gait. Julia wondered if it was some novel designer breed. A Saluki-Great Dane cross, or something.

As the girl and the dog drew level with Jono, Sean and Julia caught up with them.

'It's a goat!' said Sean, rather unnecessarily, because they could all see it quite clearly now, a tan and white goat, with short, stubby horns and little pointed hoofs. It looked at their group nervously, not sure of the dogs. The animal's pupils were shaped like slits, which gave its rather sweet, dim face an evil air, up close.

'Sit and stay,' Jono instructed the dogs in a calm tone. They obeyed immediately.

'The dogs are all right,' Jono said, as the girl hesitated to pass them. 'Nice goat.'

'Thank you. Nice dogs.'

'Thank you.' Jono smiled, proudly.

'They are very well-behaved. You've obviously trained them well.'

'I like dogs,' he said, looking down at his charges, and then up, at her face. 'Do you like goats?'

She smiled, revealing pretty, slightly skewed teeth. 'I grew up with them. My parents keep goats, and make cheese from the milk. This one's mum died and I fed her with a bottle. To cut a long story short, she's a dog now.'

Jono laughed. It was a sound, Julia realised, that she hadn't heard before. His face lit up, his frown softened and disappeared. The girl laughed too.

'At play,' Jono said, flicking his hand in the direction of the field. The dogs bolted, gambolling and chasing each other across the grass to a drift of early-autumn leaves under the oaks. Jake went in like a child dive-bombing into a swimming pool. Leo tore in after him. They wrestled and played, growling and snapping at each other in good humour.

'Ah, look how happy they are. Makes you happy to see it. I'm Laine, by the way.' As the girl spoke, she pulled at her thick dark plait, twirling the end of it, then flicked it back over her shoulder.

'Jono.'

Julia realised that the older couple should probably not be standing there watching the young ones like two dim-witted chaperones. She tugged Sean's arm gently to move him on, and walked off in the direction the dogs had taken.

'Well, that's a new one,' Sean said.

'What, Jono flirting?'

'No, a goat on a... Wait, what do you mean, he was *flirting*? Was he?'

'Er, yes, Sean. And she was flirting with him.'

'Goodness, I had no idea. Of course, you are a trained professional. An expert in interpersonal relations. That's why you can pick up the subtle clues that regular people would miss.'

'I have eyeballs in my head. It *was* pretty obvious.'

'It was? How could you tell?'

'Smiling, laughing, hair-tossing, exchange of personal information, compliments... For a start.'

Sean smiled, and made an exaggerated gesture with his head which would pass as a hair-toss if his hair wasn't thinning and cut short. 'I'm Dr Sean O'Connor, *hahaha*, and if you'll permit me to say so, you are a most attractive woman... For a start.'

'Thank heavens you're not on the market, with that flirting game,' Julia laughed and put her arm through his, pulling him close.

'Thank heavens,' he said, fervently, dropping a kiss on the top of her head.

The dogs ran to them, then back to Jono and Laine and the goat, and then back to the leaves, before finally falling into step with Julia and Sean.

'They'll be good and tired this afternoon, while we're at the funeral,' said Sean.

Nothing like the word 'funeral' to leach the good cheer from a walk, and the last warmth from the wan autumn sky. Julia looked at her watch. 'Best we get home. The funeral is at three and we have to have lunch and get changed.'

Sean looked back at Jono and Laine, who showed no sign of moving. Laine was gesturing to the goat and talking, Jono smiling and nodding. He was a good-looking young man, and his face lit up beautifully when he smiled.

'He'll come back when he's ready. Come on.'

Half of Berrywick was at Graham's funeral, including, unsurprisingly, all of the South Cotswolds Players, and all the members of the book club, who seemed to have gravitated towards each other at the back of the mourners gathered at the grave after the service. Julia and Sean had joined them. Julia gave Tabitha a quick hug and whispered a hello to Dylan, then nodded to Hector and Troilus and the others. She saw Hayley and Walter across the way, Hayley's quick eyes darting around the crowd, taking it all in. Working, Julia thought, wondering what she was looking for, specifically. Probably the same as Julia – someone who could have accessed the props cupboard with nobody noticing? The problem was that backstage is a busy place. It's hard to narrow down the possibilities without something more. There was no doubt that Hayley was thinking the same.

Looking between the rows of heads, Julia saw Graham's

family at the graveside. Jane looked dazed, as if she might have taken something to take the edge off. Hannah was next to her, holding her hand.

'Good to see Hannah has so much support,' said Tabitha, quietly, nodding towards half a dozen young women roughly Hannah's age, standing behind her, occasionally patting her on the shoulder, or offering a tissue or a bottle of water.

'They are her old school friends,' said Flo, who had slipped in next to Julia. 'I recognise some of them. They were the year above my Fiona at school. Nice that they've all come out to be with Hannah, poor lamb. Losing her father like that, and the baby so little, still.'

The baby looked back at them over Hannah's husband's shoulder, his round head bobbing on the little neck, his wide eyes a clear, untroubled blue. He would never know his grandfather. But he didn't know that, of course.

The priest invited Graham's friend and the district manager of the supermarket where Graham had been manager to say a few words, which he did in a low, rumbling voice, like rocks tumbling down a hill. He had a poetic turn of phrase. 'He was as honest as the day is long,' said the man, who had been introduced as Bill. 'He always had a kind word for anyone he met... Our customers and staff will tell you that he was always ready to give a person a chance, or a hand up... Especially those starting out in life.'

Julia had hardly known Graham, but she was quite moved to hear about his many good qualities. There was some nodding amongst the congregation, and one of the young women in front started to cry quietly, stifling little sniffs and sighs.

'He was a generous man,' Bill continued.

'True,' Flo whispered to Julia. 'He was known as a good tipper at the Buttered Scone.'

'Graham loved his family fiercely. Jane, Hannah, we know that you were the treasures of his heart.'

Jane's face was a mask. Anti-anxiety meds, was Julia's guess. Julia had always admired Jane's lively manner and elegant style. She wore her hair steely grey, in a short and stylish cut. She was always beautifully dressed, and quick with a wry comment. Today, grey-faced and dressed in black, she looked about ten years older than the woman she'd been at book club three weeks ago. She'd apparently asked for the funeral to be held as soon as possible, because she couldn't bear the idea of Graham sitting around in a morgue, and the police had released the body as there was no debate as to the manner of Graham's death.

Hannah looked like a woman who'd just walked out of a car wreck. She was motionless, but for a tear trailing down her cheek.

On the other side of the grave, towards the back of the crowd, a girl was crying as if her heart would break. Her shoulders were shaking, causing her hair to ripple prettily in the weak sunlight. When the girl turned, showing a glimpse of her face, she was familiar. Julia had seen her before, recently. That red hair was hard to forget.

'He loved the theatre, and although he died in a tragic accident, there is comfort in knowing he died on the stage, doing what he loved.'

Julia wouldn't have gone there, herself. But then, she'd seen the effects of the tragic accident up close, the big raw rip of a bullet into his chest. She tried to put the image out of her mind. Graham was at peace now, tucked into his wooden coffin, alongside the grave that would be his home for all eternity.

The priest had taken over, now. As the pallbearers lowered the coffin into the grave, a cloud moved in front of the sun, and a breeze came up. A few dead leaves skittered and rustled across the graveyard. The air was suddenly cool, and the mourners drew their coats closer against the chill. Julia pulled the collar of her jacket up to protect her neck from the breeze, and wished she'd brought a scarf. Sean put his arm over her shoulder, pulling her into his warmth.

The priest committed Graham Powell to the earth, with words that Julia always found comforting even if she didn't entirely believe them: 'In sure and certain hope of the resurrection to eternal life through our Lord Jesus Christ, we commend to Almighty God our brother Graham and we commit his body to the ground, earth to earth, ashes to ashes, dust to dust. The Lord bless him and keep him, the Lord make his face to shine upon him and be gracious unto him, the Lord lift up his countenance upon him and give him peace.'

The official ceremony over, the mourners drifted over to the church hall, where tea had been set up. Making a detour past the bathroom, Julia heard sniffing and nose blowing coming from one of the stalls. As she washed her hands in preparation for a scone, the door opened and the weeping redhead emerged. A length of thin loo paper trailed from her hand. The girl crunched it up and dampened it, and went to work on the black streaks and smudges on her face. The paper disintegrated into damp little worms and torn-off bits. Her face wasn't noticeably cleaner.

'Here you are, dear.' Julia handed her a small pack of tissues from her bag. Two-ply, quality stuff, better suited to the ravages of grief.

'Thank you,' the girl gulped, accepting the tissues.

Julia rummaged in her bag and pulled out half a roll of humbugs, which she always carried for emergencies.

'Thank you,' the girl said again, taking them. She ejected one with her thumb and popped it into her mouth, sucking hard, releasing the sweet minty smell.

'A bit of sugar always helps, at least superficially. I'm Julia.'

'I'm Bethany.'

'That's a pretty name.'

'Graham used to say that, too.' The girl looked as if she would fall back into sobs.

'I'm sorry, Bethany. It's very hard, loss. Did you know him well? Are you a friend of Hannah's?'

'Yes, I knew him well.' Her eyes welled with tears. She breathed in and out deeply to calm herself. The tears retreated. The humbug clicked against her teeth. 'Hannah and I were at school together, actually, but I was the year above. We weren't close. And then I was away for a few years, working in London. When I came back six months ago, Graham gave me a job at the shop.'

That's where Julia had seen her. She'd been outside the theatre one day, after rehearsal, waiting for Graham. She must have had a message or a delivery from work.

'Ah, I'm sorry for your loss, Bethany,' said Julia again. It always felt that all her training and years of experience were useless in the face of grief, which reduced us all to the simplest of phrases: I'm sorry. It's so hard. It gets better.

Bethany was crying again. Her tears were running clear now. Most of the mascara had already been washed away.

'I can see you were very attached to him. He must have been a good boss,' said Julia.

'A good boss? Oh, yes. Well, yes, he was, of course, people liked him. The staff. But... he... we... I don't know what I'll do now,' the young woman said sadly. 'I don't know what I'll do without him.'

She folded a fresh tissue into a stiff-edged triangle and swiped one last time beneath each eye, drawing the tears and what was left of the melted mascara from beneath the lashes, towards the outer edges of the eye. She looked at her face in the mirror and sighed, seemed to accept that was the best she could do, and tossed the tissue away in the bin.

'Thanks for the tissues, and the sweets,' she said.

'You're welcome. You take good care of yourself, Bethany.'

'I will. I think I just need to go home and have a sleep.'

'You do that. A sleep makes everything better.'

Bethany looked sceptical, as if she didn't believe it for a minute, but thanked Julia again and went on her way.

Julia was pretty peckish. She and Sean had got back from the walk with just enough time to change and eat a piece of toast before they left for the funeral. She took a plate and joined the queue at the eats table. She surveyed the funeral foods up ahead – little sandwiches, sausage rolls, cream scones, chocolate cake – weighing up the options. A whispered conversation amongst the people ahead of her entered her consciousness when she heard the word 'Bethany'. An odd coincidence, since she'd just met her. She leaned in a little, ears pricked.

'Bit of a cheek after everything,' muttered the young woman in front of Julia, shaking her head and setting the shiny blonde hair undulating.

'Selfish!' The response came as a quiet hiss of outrage.

'She always did love a drama...'

'It's just not on.'

The whisperers stopped, the women looking furtively about. One of them caught Julia's eye, and knew she'd heard them.

'The sausage rolls look good,' said the blonde at normal volume.

'Don't they just?' her friend agreed heartily. 'And I do love a sausage roll.'

'Oh, me too.'

They moved off with their plates, which each held precisely one sausage roll and a carrot stick. Julia helped herself to a sandwich, a scone, a sausage roll and a few carrots, and was pleased not to be a young woman watching her figure. She moved off to the side to wait for Sean. She wondered what to make of the conversation she'd just overheard. What had Bethany done to outrage the two young women so? Julia knew all too well how a small incident at work could get blown out of proportion. It sounded as if something like that must have happened.

Hector came and stood next to her, piled plate in hand. He stared contemplatively at the funeral crowd for a moment, then started speaking. 'I was in a funeral scene once, on *Hot Press*. How many such scenes have we seen on our screens? The weeping widow. The yawning grave. Often a mysterious figure in the background. And yet, and *yet*. Each time is the *first* time, is it not? I tried to bring that awareness to the scene when I played...'

'This isn't a television show. It's someone's actual life,' Julia snapped. It wasn't like her, but she'd had more than enough of Hector's self-involvement. 'Someone's death and someone's real life. Real grief. Not a scene in a play or a soap opera.'

'Of course, of course,' he said. 'I didn't mean to be insensitive. It's just that an actor can't help being an actor. I...'

Julia thought her head might explode if she heard the word 'I' come out of Hector's mouth one more time. Fortunately for her cranium, Sean arrived at just that moment with a plate of food. Julia turned her back on Hector to speak to Sean. 'All okay?' she asked.

'Yes. Just saying hello to a few people. Fending off bunion questions left, right and centre.'

She laughed. It was a standing joke between them that Sean could not go anywhere in Berrywick and its surrounds without bumping into a patient, and a good half of the patients he bumped into took the opportunity to ask him for a medical opinion. Very often about bunions.

'Well, I'm glad you're back. Should we go?'

'Yes,' he said.

'I'll see if I can say a quick hello and goodbye to Jane and we can be on our way.'

She waited for an old man to finish giving his condolences and let go of Jane's hand, which he'd been pressing and squeezing as if trying to wring out a damp cloth. As he turned away, Julia stepped forward. 'Jane, dear. How are you holding up? Can I bring you anything? A cup of tea, perhaps?'

'Oh, no, Julia, thank you. I'm all right. Just a bit... you know...' Jane twirled her hand at the wrist to indicate whatever it was that Julia might know, the words for which weren't coming to her at that precise moment.

'It's very hard for you, and you've done so well.'

'Thank you, Julia. It is. Very hard. So many people...' Jane looked around, seemingly bewildered.

'Well, Graham was very well-respected and loved,' said Julia. 'There might be some comfort in that.'

'He was, wasn't he?' There was something slightly off about Jane's tone when she said that. Julia sighed. There was no doubt that Jane had overdone it on the anti-anxiety meds.

'Oh yes,' Julia told Jane. 'His staff were saying how wonderful he was. They were very upset. He must have been a good employer.'

'Who?' said Jane, with a frown. She really must be more careful with the meds, Julia thought.

'Graham. A good employer.'

Jane's woozy eyes snapped into focus. 'I mean, who said that? Who was upset? One of the girls?'

'Yes, one of the girls. A few of them, I'm sure,' said Julia.

'A *few* of the work girls?' Jane looked distressed.

'Yes. Now, you look after yourself, Jane. Get a good night's sleep. And I'll come and see you during the week.'

15

When Wilma announced that it was time for tea and scones after a busy morning sorting stock at Second Chances, Julia was more than ready for a break. She'd come in on a Friday especially to help with the enormous donation that they had received from the estate of an elderly woman who had lived several miles outside of Berrywick. They'd received boxes of things from the attic of her home – including scrapbooks and clothes and toys and even a guitar covered in stickers. But it seemed that nobody had dusted the boxes or sorted the goods before sending them off to Second Chances. It always made Julia a bit melancholy to see people's precious possessions given away without a second thought.

She washed her hands, the soapy water running grey from the dust, and put the scones on a plate. Diane made the tea, and brought three mugs to the counter. When they came out from the storeroom, Wilma was doing calf-raises at the counter, lifting herself up on her toes, then down again, her left arm with its chunky sports watch swinging at her side. She was trying to rack up more steps on the step-counter app! Diane and Julia pretended not to have noticed, and Wilma pretended she hadn't seen them noticing. It was in everyone's best interests.

As part of her not-noticing act, Julia gazed fixedly out of the window, taking a close interest in the passing parade while chewing a scone, contemplatively. There was an ancient man in a tweed jacket walking a Scottie dog in a matching tweed jacket. There was a teenager on a bicycle, both hands off the handlebars, sending a text message as he pedalled along. There was a couple on the far side of the road, walking slowly, heads down in deep conversation. The man was closer to Julia, and although she couldn't see his face, she recognised something familiar about his shape and movements, even at a distance. But she couldn't place him until he lifted his head. It was Oscar! Now there was a coincidence if ever there was one. She was pleased to see that he was out in the world – she'd worried he might have gone into hibernation in his terrible state. Pure curiosity had her follow them with her eyes until they were almost out of sight.

She swallowed her last gulp of tea, jumped to her feet and said, 'Back in a minute.' She left Diane and Wilma in surprised silence, their scones poised en route to their open mouths. Once she was out on the road, Julia wasn't quite sure why she was there. She just had an instinct that she wanted to say hello to Oscar, and check up on him, but it seemed rather odd now, especially as he was with a friend. She hesitated, and watched the couple walk away from her, away from the village centre, towards the less busy periphery.

She was about to turn away when the woman tucked her hand under Oscar's arm, and held him as they walked. It was an intimate gesture. Or was it a supportive, steadying one? Julia was pondering this when the couple stopped at a corner. The woman momentarily turned towards Oscar, showing her profile to Julia for the first time. It was, unmistakably, Jane Powell! Julia watched her say a few words to Oscar and give him a goodbye kiss. Then she crossed the road and walked away.

Jane Powell kissing Oscar goodbye the day after her husband's funeral. That certainly wasn't a sight that Julia could have predicted. It nagged at her, and so she continued after Oscar. He was a good way ahead of her, and even walking at a fast pace, she caught up slowly. Her breath was coming quite heavily, she was almost panting, and it was distracting her from her thoughts about Oscar and Jane.

She didn't know what to think. Was it strange that they should be out and about together, the day after the funeral of Jane's husband, who had died at Oscar's hand, so to speak? Of course not. They had known each other for years, after all. And they had shared the same trauma, although in very different ways.

Earlier that week, when Oscar had been ranting and raving about being the murderer, Julia had been quite sure he wasn't. But now she wasn't so sure. Had it been an elaborate ruse to turn attention away from the possibility that he was telling the truth? Was there still a spark between Oscar and Jane, that he had decided to take extreme steps to reignite?

After a minute or two Julia was close enough to call out to Oscar. She put her cupped hand to her mouth, but stopped when she saw him enter Blooming Marvels, the local florist. Julia slowed her pace as she neared the pots that were artfully arranged along the pavement, and the baskets hanging from hooks on the front wall. They were a glorious sight, whatever the season, bursting with a profusion of colourful flowers and trailing plants. She was hesitant to follow Oscar into the shop. She dithered outside, admiring the pansies with their cheerful little faces. They had not a care in the world, she mused.

The decision of whether or not to speak to him was taken out of her hands by Oscar, who emerged from the shop.

'Julia!' he said. 'What a coincidence. Are you buying flowers?'

'Oh no. Not buying flowers. Just passing by. A coincidence, yes. And you? Buying flowers?'

She noticed that his hands were empty.

'Yes,' he said, offering no further information, just a shy grin.

'How are you feeling?'

'Better, I think. My talk to Dr O'Connor helped.'

'Good, Oscar, I'm glad. I hope you feel better.'

'It's all been a terrible shock, that's all. But in the end, it will all be for the best,' said Oscar, somewhat cryptically. Before Julia could ask him what he meant, he gave a little wave. 'Goodbye, then, Julia. Thanks for all your help.' Oscar turned back the way they'd come, back to the village, and his house. Julia looked at her watch. She'd been gone from Second Chances for fifteen minutes. Wilma would be wondering what on earth she was up to. She should really get back. But first...

Angela was behind the long wooden trestle table that ran almost the width of the little shop and served as desk and workbench. She was dressed, as usual, in a stylishly distressed pale denim work apron, her blonde hair in a low ponytail, tied with a piece of straw twine. She greeted Julia without ceasing her work, picking up a lily from a selection in a bucket on the table next to her and pushing it into the arrangement she was making. Next, she picked up a sprig of russet leaves. Her method seemed entirely random; in fact she hardly seemed to be looking when she reached for the next flower, or decided where to put it.

'There you go, I reckon that's about right,' she said. Her arrangement looked perfect, fresh and loose and wild, a chaotic mix of foliage, grass and flowers. 'All ready to be delivered straight to the lucky recipient.'

'Someone's going to be very happy with that,' said Julia. 'It's marvellous.'

'Pretty, isn't it? What do you think of those huge pale hydrangeas? They're a new strain, just came in a few weeks ago. I was just saying to the previous customer that I've been using them in everything, I can't get enough of them. So he's getting one in the delivery he ordered, too.'

'Oscar?'

'Yes, Oscar. Sweet chap, and a good customer.'

'I'll just pop the card on the bunch, and then I'll help you,' said Angela, patting the workbench, looking for something. 'Now, where's the card? He put it down here not a minute ago.'

A corner of paper sticking out from under a basket of grasses caught Julia's eye. 'Is this it?' she said, pushing the basket off what turned out to be a small rectangle of cardboard with a few words in a small, angular hand. She made out a capital J at the top and his name, Oscar, at the bottom, with an X below it, before Angela scooped it up.

'There we have it,' she said, pushing the card into a little envelope with the Blooming Marvels daisy logo on it, and a couple of lines of writing which Julia assumed must be an address.

'Now, what can I do for you?' asked Angela. 'Special occasion? Gift?'

'Um...' said Julia. 'No occasion. Just something cheerful for the house. Something like what you did for Oscar would be perfect.'

16

'I treated myself,' Julia told Jake, who was sitting at her feet, watching her arrange her flowers in a large glass vase. 'Arranging' was a bit of an overstatement, because they fell naturally into a lovely loose design. Nothing much further was required, and the fiddling and fluffing up was more out of habit and for her own pleasure, than for necessity. Julia knew that she sounded a little defensive. She lived comfortably but fairly frugally, and didn't often buy extravagant non-necessities. And Blooming Marvels priced its wares for London solicitors with weekend places in the Cotswolds, not retired social workers.

Jake gazed at her in adoration, as usual. He thought she'd made a great decision. In fact, he thought she deserved *more* treats. Preferably edible ones. Sausages would be nice.

She wondered where the other, almost identical, bunch of flowers had ended up. The one Oscar had bought to send to someone. Who was the J to whom the note had been addressed? Was it Jane? Or were they for some other woman? A girlfriend, perhaps? Or just a friend, someone who had done him a kindness in this time of trouble? A Jackie or a Jennifer or a Joanne.

Julia thought back to the sighting of Jane and Oscar, the

way they had leaned into each other, speaking softly. Julia thought of Jane's hand on Oscar's arm. It had seemed comfortable, a familiar gesture.

And then there was the kiss.

Julia tried to recreate the scene in her mind, to remember exactly what she had seen in that moment that Jane had turned towards Oscar and kissed him. Had it been on the cheek? Julia thought so. If Jane's lips had touched Oscar's, it would have been just a glancing touch. It hadn't been a smooch, that was for sure. But there had been something intimate about the whole scene – her hand on his arm, the kiss goodbye. Was it the intimacy of old friends? Or something more? Were Oscar and Jane involved, as they had been in the past? Was that why Graham had died? It didn't bear thinking about.

The question was whether this was something Julia needed to talk to Hayley about. Hayley might well know about the history between Jane and Oscar, but she wouldn't know how close they were now. The way the two of them had walked, and that kiss – it was two people who were very familiar with each other. And the flowers that Oscar was sending to 'J'. It could only be Jane. Then there was Oscar's strange, cryptic statement about it all being for the best. Plus, Angela had said that Oscar was a good customer, so perhaps this had been going on for some time. While Hayley might not welcome Julia's opinions on this, she had to know or she might miss something important about this case. Julia had no choice, she realised. This was more than gossip; this could be a clue. A clue that could lead to a killer, and get Julia and Tabitha cleared of any suspicion at all.

Hayley Gibson answered the call on the second ring with a rather gruff 'Julia'. Julia, who had been expecting a bit of a longer ring, and then the usual niceties – a 'hello' at least – was flustered.

'Oh, Hayley. Yes. Hello. Hayley, I've had a thought...'

'Is it a thought about a steak pie? Because I've had not a bite to eat since breakfast, and I'm finally on my way out of the office, so a steak pie is pretty much the only thought I'm interested in hearing right now.'

'It's a thought about Oscar.'

There was a pause, in which Julia heard Hayley open the car door, get in and slam the door. Her phone must have connected to the car, because Julia heard the engine start, and Hayley's echoing voice: 'What was that you were saying, Julia? I didn't hear that last thing.'

Julia decided to go with the pie, and not mention Oscar at this point.

'I was saying that I happen to have a steak pie in the freezer. If you like, I can pop it straight into the oven. You can come by, we'll chat about the other things while we eat the pie.'

On the other end of the phone, Hayley was weighing up her options.

'What other things?' she asked, suspiciously.

'I'll tell you when you get here. I'm going to put the oven on. See you soon.'

Hayley sighed. 'Okay. On my way.'

By the time the doorbell rang, the pie was in the oven, and Julia had the makings of a salad on the chopping board. A jug of home-made lemonade and two glasses stood on the table. It was early to eat dinner – not much after five – but the days were getting shorter and Hayley was hungry. Needs must, as Julia's mother always used to say.

'Hello,' Julia said, as she opened the door.

Somewhat surprisingly – as she'd not mentioned him – Hayley was accompanied by a stocky young man in black jeans and a black leather biker's jacket. This was an unusual turn of events. In the time she and Julia had known each other, Hayley had never brought a date, or in fact discussed her romantic life at all. Julia knew Hayley lived alone, but there was never a mention of a partner, or even an occasional date. A couple of gentle enquiries from Julia had been left hanging, or answered with a vague and non-specific dismissal: 'Oh, it's been a while since there was anyone special.' Julia realised that Hayley's lack of disclosure had been so effective that she had no idea whether the last someone special had been months, years or decades ago, or whether they were male or female. Julia had always thought female, but now, here was this fellow, who must have been a good ten years younger than Hayley – not that Julia was judging. Each to their own. He stood patiently, a step behind Hayley. Gosh, was he the one who had given her that beautiful orchid? He must be!

'Oh, hello!' Julia said eagerly, as if she'd been expecting him, too. She would have to set another place. 'You are very welcome, come on in.'

Hayley went inside, without so much as introducing her friend, who she left standing stiffly on the doorstep. Really, that detective was a strange one. Julia smiled at him warmly. 'Julia Bird,' she said, offering him her hand. 'I'm very pleased to meet you.'

'Um, Brian,' he said. Instead of shaking her outstretched hand, he offered her a bunch of flowers.

'These are gorgeous,' she said, admiring the pale hydrangeas and pretty blooms and grasses that were, in fact, exactly the same as the ones she had bought at Blooming Marvels. They would have to sit in the kitchen, she decided. She couldn't have Hayley's friend see that she already had the same bunch, arranged in the sitting room.

She stepped back to encourage him into the house. He seemed terribly awkward, teetering there at the threshold. And *terribly* young.

'Really, so kind of you, Brian. You didn't have to bring flowers.'

Yes, each to their own, but goodness, in the better light, she saw he must still be in his twenties. Oh, God, could she have misread the situation? Could he be someone else? Hayley's brother, perhaps? But she was only aware of a sister, who she'd met when Hayley was laid up with a broken leg.

'Um, I *did* have to?' he said, not budging, and now looking nervously from side to side, as if someone might come and rescue him from this peculiar situation. 'I'm, like, the delivery guy from the florist? It's my job, y'know? Can you sign, please?'

He held a pen and a delivery book out to her. *Blooming Marvels*, it said.

Julia could feel her face turn the fiery shade of a geranium, or a rose, or perhaps a Flanders poppy. She was pleased to be able to lower it and stare intently at the paper, while she scrawled her name.

'Thanks, Brian,' she said, handing over the pen, and shutting the door.

'Those are nice, what's the occasion?' Hayley asked. She had already sat herself at the kitchen table and poured herself a glass of the home-made lemonade. Chaplin had taken the opportunity to occupy her lap without so much as a by-your-leave, while Jake, who loved Hayley Gibson with his heart and soul, and who would ordinarily have rested his own head on her knee, looked on sadly from a distance.

'None, as far as I'm aware.'

'Is Sean one of those men who just sends you flowers for nothing? Just to be nice?' The question came out somewhere between wistful and sarcastic.

Julia took a somewhat panicky mental inventory of her relationship with Sean, in case it was the anniversary of their first date, or something. She wasn't very observant about that sort of thing, but she couldn't think of anything that might warrant sending flowers.

'I don't even know if they're from him,' she said.

'You mean there are other candidates? My word, Julia Bird. You are a dark horse!'

Instead of answering the teasing, Julia gave a stiff laugh and opened the envelope. She took out the little card, already knowing what she would find.

The large looping first letter – the J – told her that her instinct had been correct.

Julia,

Thank you for being a good friend.

Oscar

X

Julia took out a big stoneware jug and filled it with water. She pulled the twine off the flowers and plonked them into the jug without explanation. For the second time today she fluffed and fiddled unnecessarily with a bunch of blooms. She was playing for time while her mind turned over the events of the day, and what they all meant. The recipient of Oscar's flower purchase was not, as she'd suspected, Jane, but Julia herself. They were nothing more than a generous thank you gift.

Did that change anything? She had seen Jane and Oscar, their familiarity, their intimate gestures. Her hand on his arm. The kiss. The odd statement.

'So, are they from Sean?'

'Actually, no.'

'Well, who are they from? What does the card say?' Hayley asked. She seldom asked personal questions, but her detective brain loved a mystery. She clearly couldn't resist the question.

'They're from Oscar.'

Hayley didn't say anything, just stroked the cat with a rhythmic gesture. Julia was reminded of the villain in James Bond, the one with the fluffy Persian on his lap.

When the silence got too much, Julia said, 'They're only a thank you gift for helping him yesterday.'

She put the jug of flowers on the kitchen table.

'The pie will be ready in about ten minutes,' she said. And then blurted, because she couldn't bear the silence and the stroking of the cat, 'I saw Oscar and Jane together.'

'You did?'

'Yes. They were walking down the road. She had her hand on his arm. Linked, sort of. And they were talking. Quite seriously, you know. Heads down.'

'I see. And how did they...?'

'And then she kissed him.'

'A long kiss? Like a smooch?'

'I wouldn't say a smooch. They were on a public road.' Julia was aware of sounding like a Mother Grundy. 'What happened was, they were walking together, arm in arm, talking, and they got to the intersection. She was going one way and he the other, and they kissed goodbye.'

'Ah, well, a kiss goodbye.'

'That's different, isn't it? From a *kiss* kiss, I mean. That's what I thought, too. But I thought I should mention it to you anyway. As the investigator.'

'On the mouth or the cheek?'

'The kiss? I don't know. It seemed like mostly the cheek, but perhaps somewhere in between.'

'But not lingering.'

'No. Not lingering. But not a peck on the cheek, either.'

'Her husband was killed just a week ago.'

'I know. I was there. I'm sure it's nothing.'

Hayley made a *hhhmmph* sound.

The oven timer made a *brrriiinnnggg* sound.

Julia's phone made a *diddly-dee* sound.

A message had arrived.

17

Julia always spent a few minutes on a Monday morning planning her week. While feeding the cat, the dog and the chickens, she ran through her social plans and other commitments in her head. Over her second cup of tea, she listed, on a piece of paper this time, the errands she had to run, the admin tasks requiring attention, and the chores in the house and garden that she would complete.

She paused and looked at the list. She was aware that her schedule was only lightly sprinkled with activities, and that most of these were very minor. Still, they somehow filled her days and kept her surprisingly busy and fulfilled. She wondered if *A Night to Remember* would lurch back into production, and require her presence this week, or whether Roger would finally admit defeat. From the silence from most people on the WhatsApp group, it seemed that enthusiasm for the idea of the amdram festival might be diminishing – other than with Hector, of course. He seemed undeterred, as far as the production was concerned, and had been sending messages on the WhatsApp group since Friday, asking when the next rehearsal would be.

Julia grabbed her keys and decided to get a start on the list.

'All right then, you can come for the ride,' she told Jake, who was pacing about eagerly in the hope of an outing. He didn't have to be asked twice. She opened the front door and he shot out like a bullet from a gun, to sit expectantly next to the car. She opened the car's back door and he was inside in an instant, sitting solemnly upright as he always did, like an important fellow being ferried around town by his chauffeur.

The two books Julia needed to deliver to Hayley were on the passenger seat next to her. She would drop them off first, she decided. One easy tick for the to-do list! There was a parking space right outside the police station. She opened Jake's window and instructed, 'Be good. I won't be a minute.' He assured her, mutely, that he would indeed be good.

A tall, besuited man came down the pavement and walked into the station just ahead of Julia. His grey hair looked as if it had been cut that very morning, or perhaps every morning. Every hair was in place. He approached Cherise, at the front desk, with an officious air. Julia hung back a few paces, so as not to intrude.

'Garfield Lineker. Solicitor,' he said. 'I need to see Detective Inspector' – he consulted a piece of paper, which he'd taken from his pocket – 'Gibson. Hayley Gibson. It's in connection with Graham Powell.'

Julia inched forward, very smoothly, so as not to draw attention to herself.

'I'm afraid the detective is in a meeting,' said Cherise. 'Can I give her a message for you?'

'I need to see her in person.'

'Ah, well, you can wait, or I can ask her to phone you?'

'It's important. Please let her know I'm here.'

Julia watched Cherise's eyes narrow slightly. She was not a woman to be trifled with, Cherise. She'd been at Berrywick police station for ten years and she'd seen more than her fair share of entitled lawyers, not to mention singing drunks, combative neighbours, fighting spouses and worried parents.

'I'll let her know once her meeting is over. You are welcome to wait. It might be a while, though.' Cherise seemed rather pleased to be able to impart this last piece of information.

Mr Lineker leaned in. 'I am Graham Powell's lawyer. I have information that I believe may be pertinent to his death.'

'What is the nature of the information?' Cherise asked.

Julia wanted to know, too. She turned her head, so her good ear was pointed in their direction, and gazed at the noticeboard on the far wall, as if engrossed in a poster encouraging the villagers of Berrywick to *Make that call!* if they saw anything suspicious. In Julia's experience, the villagers of Berrywick didn't need a lot of encouragement.

The lawyer spoke quietly, but Julia managed to hear every word. 'I was acting for him in a particular matter, a *personal* matter. A legal letter was delivered to a certain person that very morning, the morning of his demise, and I believe this information should form part of the investigation into Mr Powell's death.'

Cherise picked up the phone and said, 'Could you come to the front desk, please?'

Mr Lineker looked very pleased with himself, having strong-armed the desk sergeant, triumphed over the system, and rustled up DI Hayley Gibson. Except that it was DC Walter Farmer who appeared, looking rather harassed.

'Oh, hello, Julia,' he said. 'What can I help you with?'

'Not Mrs Bird,' said Cherise, tossing her head in the direction of the lawyer. 'Mr... Errr?'

'Lineker.'

'Ah. Hello, I'm DC Farmer.' Walter gestured to the lawyer to follow him.

'Is DI Gibson available?'

'Come with me, sir, I'll take your statement.'

'It's very important that I see the DI. My client...'

The man's voice continued, muffled, as he followed Walter through the door, and then was heard no more. The door opened, and one of the young constables came through, along with Mr Lineker's insistent voice: '...he served her notice of intent to divorce on Saturday morning...' The door closed behind them, leaving Julia wondering.

'Mrs Bird?' The way Cherise said her name made Julia think she must have said it at least once before catching her attention.

'Sorry, Cherise. My mind wandered. I have a little something for Hayley Gibson. Some books I thought she might like. I imagine she's very busy with everything that's going on, so I don't want to bother her. But would you mind giving them to her when you see her?'

'Yes, of course.' Cherise reached over and took the books, turning them over to read the blurbs. 'Oooh, these do look nice. I think I've read one of hers. American police detectives are so much hunkier, aren't they?'

Julia did not feel it her place to comment on the relative hunkiness of American versus British police detectives, especially given the proximity of the latter. Instead, she said, 'It's an author Hayley likes. Someone brought a few newish ones into Second Chances, and I nabbed them.'

'Ah.'

'Paid for them, of course,' Julia clarified. 'I wouldn't just take them.' There was something about being in a police station, even one that Julia had come to know so well, that made Julia feel as if she might be accused of a crime at any moment.

Cherise smiled. 'Oh, of course not. I'm sure DI Gibson will be very pleased. She needs something to take her mind off things, that's for sure, other than the chocolates and flowers she keeps getting. She's been working like a madwoman, as usual. Loads of paperwork with poor Graham's death, of course. And now this.' She gestured with her head towards the door, behind which the pushy lawyer was no doubt badgering Walter Farmer for access to the senior officer. Cherise gave an almost imperceptible roll of her eyes.

'Give Hayley my best,' said Julia. 'I hope she enjoys the books.'

Julia went home via the post office – a second item ticked off the list – her head full of what she'd heard: *He served her notice of intent to divorce...* And before that, he'd said something about a personal matter, a legal letter delivered on the morning of his death. Try as she might, Julia couldn't find any interpretation of these snippets of conversation other than that Graham was planning to divorce Jane. And he'd told her on the day of his death. But what did that have to do with...

The furious blare of a car's hooter dragged Julia out of her musing. She slammed her foot on the brake, sending Jake into the back of her seat. She was shocked to find the car's nose halfway into a junction, having stopped too late.

The dog was fine, if somewhat put out. But not nearly as put out as the man shaking his fist at her. From the angle of his car, he'd skidded to a halt when she'd come through the give way sign in front of him.

'Look where you're going, you idiot!' he shouted through his rolled-down window. 'You could have killed someone.'

And the truth of it was, she could have.

Just as surely as someone had killed Graham Powell with that bullet in the prop gun and with Oscar's finger on the trigger.

18

Sean grinned a self-satisfied-trying-to-look-modest grin as he placed his coffee cake on the eats table. Although a reasonable cook, he was not much of a baker, and his previous contributions to book club tea had been rather amateurish in their execution – a wonky carrot cake that had somehow risen more on one side than the other; a chocolate cake with a dip in the middle; a plate of slightly undercooked cheese straws. This cake was symmetrical and smoothly iced, and smelled tantalisingly of fresh coffee.

'That looks incredible!' said Tabitha.

Dylan nodded approvingly. 'Proper professional.'

'I watched a video on YouTube,' Sean said. 'It was Jono's idea. He found it for me. It's quite amazing what you can get online! Step-by-step instructions, and you can see exactly what it's meant to look like at every stage.'

He seemed genuinely amazed by the existence of cooking videos, as did Tabitha.

'Really?' she said. 'I can see how that would be useful. I always feel nervous when I read "beat until stiff peaks form".'

'Yes, or "until smooth and glossy".'

'What even is that? Glossy?'

'And then there's "bake until golden".'

'Exactly. I start to doubt myself. I mean, is it really golden, or is that more like light brown?'

'That's the beauty of the videos,' said Sean. 'You can see the exact colour it's meant to be.'

Dylan smiled at this exchange, which probably sounded like something from medieval times to him. Julia had come late to baking – her ex-husband Peter had been the cook in their marriage – but when she had, she had just followed the recipes and hoped for the best without overthinking it. She certainly didn't try to differentiate between shades of gold and light brown. Her offerings might not be professional level, but it was her experience that fresh-baked foods were always appreciated and generally wolfed down, even if they were a little rough around the edges.

Pippa came in, looking flustered, her blonde ponytail askew. 'Sorry I'm late. One of the puppies ate a plastic dinosaur that my friend's child dropped...'

'What sort of dinosaur? Was it a diplodocus?' asked Dylan. 'A stegosaurus?'

'I have absolutely no idea, but I had to wait and see if it appeared and then...' She surveyed the appalled faces of the book lovers and said, 'Never mind.'

She settled into a comfortable armchair with a happy sigh.

Diane arrived on the very dot of six thirty. 'Made it!' she said, plonking her bag of books onto an empty seat.

The book club members were all there except for Jane, whose absence was hardly surprising.

'I think this is us, for today. Let's get seated and start, shall we?' said Tabitha.

They found seats, settling in with their books, ready for discussion. The library cat, who went by the name Too, sashayed in and looked around the assembled group, as if deciding who to favour with her company. Clearly, no lap was to her liking that day, because she looked mildly pained and took up a position on the floor in the centre of the circle, where she could be easily admired by everyone present while she groomed her tail with long, determined licks of her pink tongue.

'Did you hear about Jane?' asked Diane, before Tabitha could kick things off.

This wasn't a sufficiently precise question, given what had happened to Jane recently. They all looked at Diane expectantly for further information.

'After all she's been through, the poor woman, losing her husband like that,' said Diane, her already somewhat bulbous eyes growing rounder. The book clubbers waited expectantly. 'She's been taken in for questioning by the police.'

Julia's blood ran cold. This had to be something to do with that lawyer who'd turned up this morning, talking about the divorce papers.

'For questioning?' asked Pippa. 'Surely not.'

'Surely yes. My sister's friend lives next door to Jane. She was visiting Jane when Jane got the call from that young fella, Walter.'

'I mean, they can't imagine she had anything to do with what happened.'

'Of course not!' said Diane. 'It's not possible. I don't understand what the police are thinking.'

'I'm sure the Berrywick police have everything under control. They probably just need more information,' said Tabitha.

'At 5.02 p.m.?' said Diane, whose information was clearly up to the minute.

'Justice never sleeps, yeah?' said Dylan, as if 5.02 p.m. was the middle of the night.

'Julia?' said Diane.

'What?'

'You know all about police things. You know the detectives. And you know Jane. Can't you do something?'

'Diane, I agree with Tabitha,' Julia said. 'We must let the police do their job.'

'Yes, but Jane isn't...'

'Come on now,' said Tabitha. 'I know we're all very concerned about Jane's well-being, and about finding answers to what happened to Graham. But the only thing we can do right now is to be together, and get on with our book club meeting. So. Shall we?'

Diane hesitated for a moment, sending a final pleading look Julia's way, then settled back into her chair. 'Okay then. You're right, Tabitha. Books. Well, I must say, I enjoyed this memoir of a French woman who lived with the elephants in South Africa.' She held up the book for inspection, and talk turned to elephants, and the African bush, and adventure, and brave women. Julia's mind was elsewhere, though. At a lawyer's office, where papers had been in the process of being drawn up to end a marriage. A marriage that had come to an end in a different, unexpected way, just twenty-four hours later.

At the end of book club, Julia said her goodbyes and left, nicely full of coffee cake, and with a tote bag full of books over her shoulder. Sean walked out with her. They stood on the pavement in air just chilly enough to turn their breath visible.

'Sorry I can't stay over,' Sean said. 'I need to get back to Jono.'

'I quite understand. Perhaps we can get together at the weekend... Or the following weekend, if that's better.'

'Yes. I'd like that. It's just that I'm at work all day, so I'm just giving him some time with having me, you know... around, in the evenings. We'll have more time together when he's a bit more settled.'

'Sean,' she took his hand, and spoke softly. 'There's no pressure. Of course I want to see you, but I am absolutely willing to wait until you think the time is right. You must do what's best for Jono, and for your relationship with him.'

'Thank you. I do worry. He's quite vulnerable, I think. And it sounds like he's been drinking a lot. Not now, but when he was in London. He had the most frightful hangover when I collected him. I'm trying to encourage him to see a professional. A doctor or a psychologist. He's always resisted, but he's a bit more open to it now. He can see he needs help. I'm hopeful that while he's here, he'll agree.'

'I can see he's calmer already. Being with you is grounding; it's good for him.'

'I think it's being with Leo that calms him.' Sean laughed, but Julia could tell he was only half joking.

'He's brilliant with dogs.'

'If he had to deal with dogs instead of people, he'd be just fine, that boy of mine.'

There was something wistful and sad in Sean's tone, but he rallied quickly, with rather forced good cheer. 'Well, I'd best be getting home. Drive safe, love.'

'You too. Chat in the morning.'

19

Julia picked up her phone to do the Wordle while she waited for the tea to brew, and saw she had a missed call. A phone call from an unknown number was a rare occurrence, and it always gave her a funny anxious feeling. This particular mystery was quickly solved by the text message: *Hello Mrs Bird. It's Hannah here, Jane's daughter. I tried to phone. It's about my mum. Please give me a call as soon as you can. Thanks. Hannah*

Hannah picked up the phone on the second ring. She must have been waiting with it in her hand.

'Thank you for phoning back, Mrs Bird.' She sounded relieved, as if she had been holding her breath and could now let it out. 'I'm sorry to phone so early, but it's about my mum. The police came yesterday afternoon and asked her to come in and answer some questions. They kept her overnight. I had to take her a bag. I've called her lawyer, but Mum told me to get hold of you for her.'

'Me?'

'Yes, you. Julia Bird. She said you're a sensible woman and you understand the system. She said you would know what to do.'

Julia was positively flummoxed at this turn of events. She did not, at all, know what to do. She didn't even know what to say.

'Will you help us, Mrs Bird? I wouldn't ask, but I'm here with the baby and I don't know who to speak to about anything. My husband's gone to London for work. My dad is gone. And now my mum... I wouldn't ask, but... will you help me?'

Julia sighed, inwardly. She knew that there was only ever one answer to that question, whether she liked it or not.

'I'd like to help you, Hannah, and I'm sorry for your troubles, but I'm not sure what, if anything...'

'Please. I don't know who else to ask. Can we just meet for coffee? The Buttered Scone?'

Julia really, really wished she could just say no, but just saying no wasn't in her nature. She thought of poor Hannah, alone with baby Tom. And poor Jane in jail overnight.

'Just a coffee?' Hannah said, her voice catching.

'Of course. I'll see you there at eleven. And please, call me Julia.'

The Buttered Scone was already humming with customers, many of them out-of-towners on a day trip or a weekend away, enjoying the pretty villages of the Cotswolds. Of which Berrywick was one of the prettiest, and somewhat less overrun than some of the others. Summer was the high season for visitors, but in Julia's opinion, this early autumn was just as lovely, maybe more so, with the trees turning their golds and reds, the light bright and soft, and the villages not too busy.

Julia found a table in the window, where she could keep an eye out for Hannah, and sat down. She was, as usual, about three minutes early. 'It's a curse,' she said to Jake, who had plonked his bottom down on the floor next to her chair, and was looking up at her expectantly. 'I've tried to be late, but I can't.'

She really wished she hadn't weakened and agreed to meet Hannah. It seemed like a meeting with a high chance of something going wrong. Julia didn't know how much Hannah knew about her parents' relationship, which seemed, increasingly, to have been more troubled than one might have imagined. Jane certainly seemed to be close to Oscar, her old friend, from what Julia had seen of the two of them together. Had *that* been the cause of the impending divorce? Was Jane involved with Oscar? If so, the police had good reason to be questioning Jane.

Or had Graham had his own reasons for wanting out of the marriage?

Julia thought back to the funeral, and the weeping woman who had worked for him, the mascara-smeared girl she'd seen in the ladies'. Bethany, that was her name. Her colleagues hadn't had a kind word for her, that's for sure. In fact, they had implied that she had a cheek being at the funeral at all. Was it perhaps Graham who had been having the affair – and with young Bethany, at that? Either way, speaking to Hannah would be a minefield.

Julia saw something that stopped her thoughts in their tracks. As if by some strange conjuring trick of the universe, Bethany herself had materialised next to Julia's table. She looked down at Julia, first with a moment of confusion, as if trying to remember when they'd met, and then with a nod of recognition. She turned quickly away from her, as if avoiding any possible interaction, and walked towards the door, followed closely by none other than Superintendent Roger Grave.

He walked behind Bethany, carrying her wrap, which he laid tenderly over her shoulders as they stepped outside the Buttered Scone. He turned her to face him and pulled the shawl up, tucking it around her neck, as one might tuck a child into bed. With his hands on her shoulders, he looked deeply into her eyes, and pulled her quickly to him for a hug.

Well, this was a turn-up for the books.

Julia's head was spinning, considering all the seemingly contradictory possibilities. Had Bethany been involved with Graham *and* with Roger? Did she have not one, but *two* older suitors? Had the two men known about each other? There was so much Julia couldn't comprehend. Aside from anything else, the young just had so much *energy*.

'That Bethany, who'd have thought?' said Flo, who had appeared quietly, in her silent plimsolls, and was following Julia's gaze. Julia looked at Flo expectantly, awaiting elaboration.

'I'm not one to gossip.'

This could not be further from the truth, but Julia let it pass. She held her silence, waiting for Flo to crack.

'It's nice to see them so friendly together, her and the superintendent. So affectionate. I wouldn't have thought it possible, things being so smooth now. Not after the way the relationship ended. Sparks flew, I can tell you. Not surprising. Too young, of course. That was the problem.'

'Yes, very young.' It was increasingly difficult to determine the age of young people, but Julia reckoned Bethany couldn't have been more than thirty. Probably less. Roger could be twice her age.

'Still, life surprises you, doesn't it? Look at the two of them now.'

They watched through the window as the couple said their goodbyes with another hug, and went their separate ways. They walked a few steps away from each other, and both turned at exactly the same moment. They smiled and waved at each other, turned again and continued on their way.

'Ah, will you look at that,' said Flo, mistily. 'Isn't that nice?' Julia was surprised that Flo was so in favour of this romantic pairing. In fact, she seemed quite moved by it, despite the age gap. And what about the fact that she said it had ended badly? Yet here they were together. It was all rather odd.

'Coffee for you, is it, Julia?'

'Yes please, Flo, and I'll wait to order food.'

Minutes later, Hannah came in, pushing the baby in the pram. Julia stood up to help her navigate through the chairs.

'Thanks,' said Hannah, puffed. 'It doesn't exactly have great manoeuvrability. It's like driving a ship.'

'Through icebergs,' said Julia, moving a chair out of the way.

Baby Tom sat propped up, like the ship's very small commander, surveying the floes and bergs as he sailed past. He seemed content with the whole arrangement.

'Thank you for meeting me. I know it's a lot to ask.'

'I'm sorry for the loss of your dad, Hannah, and now this difficulty with your mum. I'm just not sure what I can do to help. I suspect there's a lot going on that I don't know.'

Hannah was quiet for a minute, and then said, 'I feel I can trust you. I'm going to tell you something I don't want everyone to know. My father was having an extramarital relationship when he was killed. It was with a young woman at the supermarket. Actually, someone I was at school with. I feel awful. It was my fault. I recommended her for the job, and then she and Dad...'

Hannah looked down at Tom, and then leaned towards Julia and whispered, as if not wanting the baby to hear, 'They were having an affair.'

'Coffee for you, Julia. And there's a little something for Jake,' Flo put down the cup and, next to it, a separate saucer with three bone-shaped dog biscuits on it. Julia found it amusing that they shaped biscuits like bones. They could have been shaped like elephants or steam trains and it wouldn't make a blind bit of difference to Jake.

'Now, what can I get for you, Hannah dear?'

'Tea please, Flo.'

When Flo was out of earshot, Julia asked quietly, 'Did Jane... did your mother know about the affair?'

'She did. I'm not sure when she found out, exactly, but she didn't tell me, or anyone, as far as I know. She didn't want people to know. You know what my mum is like; she's a proud woman, and sort of, like, proper. And Berrywick is a small village when it comes to gossip. I think she was hoping that before anyone got wind of it, the relationship would blow over and things would just go back to normal.'

That would be a highly unusual outcome, in Julia's experience. And it certainly hadn't worked out that way in this case.

'Dad was hesitating, apparently. He said wanted to try again, but then there was this young woman, and you know men... He went back and forth for a bit, and then just last week he made a decision. He wanted to split up. He wanted to be with Bethany. He had his lawyer draw something up to send to Mum, a preliminary sort of thing, I suppose. Mum got the letter the day he died.'

Julia knew this, of course, but she didn't say so. Just nodded in a sympathetic sort of way.

'Mum's mistake was that she didn't tell the police when they first questioned her. She thought, well, it doesn't matter now that he's... gone. The affair was not relevant, and the least she could do was protect his reputation, and our family's. But when they found out, it made her look... shifty.'

Guilty, more like, thought Julia.

'And now they've brought her in for questioning.'

'Hannah, it doesn't necessarily mean they think she was... responsible for Graham's death. It's more that they want to see if she has more information.'

'But they questioned her and questioned her, and kept her there overnight. She's with them as we speak. God knows what she's going through.'

Hannah got tearful at this, as if imagining the gentle Berrywick police waterboarding a confession out of Jane.

A pot of tea appeared in front of Hannah, along with a cup

and saucer and a small jug of milk. 'And I thought you could use a muffin, dear; you are looking a bit peaky and you must keep your strength up for that baby, now,' Flo said kindly, placing it next to her. 'It's on the house.'

'Thank you, Flo, you are very kind.'

When they were alone again, Julia continued: 'Hannah, your mum made a mistake withholding information. When the police find out a person is not being forthcoming, they tend to be a bit more suspicious, a little less friendly.'

'Poor Mum, after all she's been through. I know she made a mistake, but it's so wrong.'

Julia pushed the little red teapot towards the young woman. 'Have a bit of tea, now, dear. And put some sugar in it. She'll be out any minute. They'll realise she made a mistake and let her go. They're not going to hold a grieving widow who's done nothing wrong.'

As a statement, this was true. The police wouldn't hold a newly widowed, innocent woman who had done nothing wrong. But *had* Jane done nothing wrong? Julia didn't think Jane was a murderer, but neither could she say that she was a hundred per cent certain of it. Jane's relationship with Oscar; Graham's with Bethany. The divorce papers that were delivered *on the same day* as the murder.

And right then, Julia realised with a pounding heart that she had a piece of information that Hannah certainly did not know.

20

It was with some ambivalence that Julia found herself parked outside the Berrywick police station, dithering. On the one hand, Hannah and the book club were counting on Julia to come to Jane's defence. There was also Julia's own fondness for the Jane she knew from book club – a smart woman and insightful reader, who had exhibited nothing but decency and good-heartedness in the years they'd known each other.

But what had actually brought Julia to the station this morning was that other very specific piece of information that she had remembered, with a cold shiver, while talking to Hannah at the Buttered Scone. It might be nothing, but she felt Hayley needed to know. It was a piece of information that would have the exact opposite effect from what Hannah and the book club had hoped for. It would make Jane look like a more, rather than less, likely suspect.

What Julia knew was that Jane had been in that props cupboard on the day of the play opening. She'd had the opportunity to meddle with the gun. Yes, she had been returning Graham's fake moustache, but who's to say that wasn't a cover story? She might have used the opportunity to plant the bullet, and wipe her prints off the gun. Could Jane have planned the whole thing to kill her philandering husband? And, if so, could Oscar have been in on it?

Julia remembered that she had been with Roger when they'd made this realisation. But they'd been interrupted by the call about the fingerprints. Julia couldn't be sure that in the discussions around the missing prints, Roger would ever have mentioned to Hayley that Jane had dropped off the moustache. That detail might well have got lost in the bigger picture of the fingerprints on the prop gun.

There was only one thing for it – she needed to ask him, and if he hadn't said anything, she needed to tell Hayley. She hoped that she would find Roger at the police station, or that they would know where he was.

'You're going to have to stay in the car,' she said to Jake, who was sitting up expectantly. 'I'm popping into the police station. I won't be a moment, and I'll leave all the windows open. No chewing the seat belt.' This last, she said sternly. She'd already had to replace one of the back seat belts, although that had been a while ago and Jake had mostly stopped his chewing habit since then. 'If you're a very good boy and I'm quick, we might get to see Leo and Jono later, okay?'

Jake seemed to accept the bargain. He watched her close the door, then gave a resigned sigh and flopped down onto the back seat for a quiet snooze. Julia heard footsteps gaining on her as she neared the door to the police station.

'Julia.'

She turned. It was Oscar.

'Goodness, Oscar, well, I didn't expect to see you here.'

That was an understatement. If Jane and Oscar had been seeing each other when Jane's husband was killed, pitching up at the police station where she was being questioned seemed like a bold move on Oscar's part.

'I'm here for Jane, of course.'

Oh dear, the foolishness of love. How many times had Julia seen it end in pain and disaster, even death?

'Is that sensible, Oscar?' asked Julia. 'It might be a bit surprising to the police.' She hoped she'd worded this diplomatically.

'I am the family lawyer, so it's hardly surprising I'm here.'

'The family lawyer? Oh, I didn't know.'

She had known he was a lawyer, of course. But not that Jane was his client.

That might explain everything – especially if Jane's marriage had been falling apart. Their intense conversations could well have been professional. Playing it all over in her mind, Julia could see that there was actually very little hard evidence that pointed to anything more. Julia felt her face flush with the shame and embarrassment of her crazy assumptions.

'I've been their lawyer for years,' Oscar was saying. 'For both of them. Of course, in the last little while that has been a bit... Let's just say I'm Jane's lawyer now. She's needed rather a lot of legal advice recently.'

'I saw Graham's lawyer the other day. He was here at the police station, talking about a separation...'

Oscar looked surprised – and not in a good way – to discover that this piece of the puzzle was already out in the world.

'Yes, well, I really can't discuss anything more with you. Client confidentiality, and so on. But I'm here to help Jane in any way I can.'

'Ah, so your relationship is professional then, is it?'

'What do you mean?'

'Somehow I thought you were... friends.'

'The Powells and I go back a long way. Yes, we are friends. Jane and I have some ancient history between us. But I'm also their lawyer, a role that I take very seriously.'

'Good, well, I'm glad Jane has somebody in her corner. It seems she is in a sad and difficult situation.'

Oscar and Julia walked into the station, Julia chewing over what Oscar had told her. Did this change things, she wondered? She still needed to find out if Roger had told Hayley about the moustache. But when she asked Cherise if she could speak to Roger, Cherise told her that Roger was out for the day.

'Do you know where I might find him?' asked Julia.

'It's hardly for me to ask Superintendent Grave his movements for the day, is it?' said Cherise, glaring at Julia. Julia conceded that indeed, it was not, and that she would have to send him a text. She felt a bit awkward messaging him for police business when she only had his number because of the show. She went back to the car, thinking about what she now knew, and how it might fit in with what she had thought.

Jake was thrilled to see her back. Thrilled! The separation had been long and arduous – although, truth be told, it was five minutes and he had been asleep for its entirety – and now they were reunited. He breathed his hot, foggy dog breath onto her neck while she fastened her seat belt. She opened the driver's side window and gulped in a lungful of fresh air.

'Good chap, Jakey,' she said, having surveyed the car for new tooth marks. 'Give me a minute and we'll be on our way.'

While she had been standing in the police station speaking to Cherise, she had heard a WhatsApp message arrive on her phone. She pulled it out of her handbag to check.

It was from Roger himself to the group.

Hi all. Please see the new cast list below.

'Third time lucky,' Julia muttered to herself. Indeed, as promised, there followed a list of names of characters and names of actors. Oscar and Graham were not amongst them, of course. Hector was listed, once again, as Postman. The poor chap would be most disappointed. Julia was sorry for him, but admired Roger's resolve. Hector was indisputably a truly terrible actor. Sure, this wasn't the West End, just an amateur production in the Cotswolds, but you had to have some standards. Roger was, if nothing else, a professional – even when it came to amateur dramatics – and a sensible man.

But Roger's message was, for once, perfectly timed.

Julia typed out a message to him.

Hi Roger. Good call on the casting, Tab and I will get the props and costumes sorted. Could I chat to you about something else? Not cast-related, you'll be pleased to hear! Maybe a coffee? It's a bit urgent.

His reply was almost instant: *Are you in the village? I'll be at the hall until about 2 p.m. You can pop in if you are about.*

Yes, yes, she did want to pop in! She messaged to say she'd be round shortly and got a thumbs-up.

Jake wasn't pleased to be left in the car again, but this really was a pop-in. She opened the windows and reiterated her previous instructions, then followed the path through the garden to the hall. The big main door was locked, so she went around to the side door, adjacent to the stage. This door was open. Through the gap she saw Roger Grave's back, his long neck angled towards the phone held to his ear. She was hesitant to interrupt him, and in the moment that she hovered in the doorway she heard him say sweetly, 'Darling, you know you can rely on me. Even though I disapproved of what you planned to do, when I realised I couldn't talk you out of it, I helped you with Graham.'

Roger's voice dropped, as he walked towards the other side of the hall, and out of Julia's hearing. Julia was shocked by what she'd heard. *I helped you with Graham.* Helped who? With what? Had Roger had something to do with Graham's death?

He had called the person darling, and his tone had been so loving. Roger Grave was not, by nature, a gushing man. There was only one other time that Julia had seen him behave lovingly – with Bethany outside the Buttered Scone. She felt sure he must be speaking to Bethany now – who else could it be? If Bethany had been in a relationship with Graham, and then with Roger, maybe the two of them had felt a need to get rid of Graham. Hadn't Hector mentioned that things had been tense between the two men in rehearsals? That would certainly be true if they were fighting over the same woman. But would that lead to murder?

Roger had had even more opportunity than Jane had to load the prop gun; and Roger's fingerprints had been on the weapon. Julia had presumed it had been from when Roger had taken the gun from Oscar at the scene. But thinking about it now, a policeman of Roger's experience would have been more careful about adding prints to the weapon – unless he wanted a reason for his own prints to appear on the gun. Julia's heart started pounding. The more she thought about it, the more sense this was making.

She stepped backward, moving slowly. She didn't want to face him until she'd had more time to think about it. But Roger must have felt her presence, because he started to turn around. Julia had the presence of mind to step forward. By the time he saw her, she looked as if she'd just arrived and could not possibly have overheard him.

'Hello, Roger,' she called out with a deliberate casualness. She felt a nervous constriction in her throat, but hoped it wasn't obvious in her voice.

'Hi, Julia,' he said, holding up his hand to indicate he needed a moment. Speaking into his phone he said, 'I've got to go, Bethie. Let's chat later... Okay... You too.'

Julia smiled and gave a 'don't mind me...' wave of her hand, but inside, she was all a-churn. It *was* Bethany that he had been speaking to! She didn't have time to properly process what she had heard. That would be for later. For now, she had to think of something to say, a reason for being here.

Roger Grave was now off the phone and looking at Julia expectantly. She couldn't discuss the case with him, not after what she'd heard. She just stood there gaping, hoping that something would come to her. Nothing did.

'How are you, Julia? What can I do for you? What did you want to talk about?'

'The dogs!'

She blurted the words. They seemed to come straight out of her mouth without spending even a brief sojourn in her brain. And then she was committed.

'Dogs? I'm sorry, but you'll have to explain.'

'Yes, of course, that's what I'm going to do. I'll explain.'

She smiled and nodded like a lunatic.

'Are you all right, Julia?'

'Yes, yes. Of course. It's just the dogs, you see. I had a thought. Which seemed like a very good thought. So I thought, Roger! He's the man to talk to.'

'About the dogs?'

'Yes, let me explain...'

He waited.

'I was thinking of a fundraiser, that's it.' Julia almost laughed with relief when the idea entered her head. It was an idiotic idea, most likely, but at least she had something to work with. 'People love dogs, don't they? And Graham loved dogs.'

It was true, in fact, as far as she knew, that Graham had loved dogs. She had regularly spotted Graham and Jane at the dog park with a brace of small yappy beasts, each with a different coloured ribbon in its well-groomed hair.

Roger's expression had morphed from mildly confused

towards concerned. He must be wondering if she had had a stroke.

'A dog fundraiser?'

'Yes, that's the idea,' she said, more confidently. Now she had an idea, she gathered steam. 'I was thinking, perhaps we could do a special performance of the show as a fundraiser for the RSPCA. In Graham's memory.'

As she said it, she thought it was rather a good idea. Perhaps even brilliant.

'I like that, Julia.' Roger Grave smiled. 'We'd have to run it by Jane, of course. But I know that everyone in the group would like to do something to honour Graham.'

Especially the man who murdered him! What better cover up for his evil act? The thought came back to Julia with the force of a blow. She replayed the fragments of Roger's conversation with Bethany in her mind. *When I realised I couldn't talk you out of it, I helped you with Graham...* What else could that mean? Somehow, Bethany and Roger had orchestrated the death of Graham Powell – Bethany's love, Roger's rival for her affections.

Julia had to get out of there. 'I know you're busy, Roger, and I've left Jake in the car, so I'll be running, then. Well not running, not running away, just, I'd better be on my way. So you think about it. Think about Graham. I mean, the fundraiser, not Graham himself. And we can talk about it some other time. Okay?'

'Are you all right, Julia? You look pale and a bit... shaky.'

'Blood sugar,' she said, without further explanation.

'Sweetie?' he asked, rummaging in his jacket pockets. 'I always have a toffee on me somewhere.'

He pulled out a sweet in rather crumpled paper. Julia snatched it from his hand, just to put an end to the exchange. She unwrapped it and tossed it into her mouth.

'Thanks.' The word came out more like 'Hunks'.

The toffee must have been in his pocket since the Early Jurassic, and was approximately as hard as the rocks from the same era. This was helpful, in fact. She made muffled sounds and a series of mimed movements in place of a proper goodbye, and made a hasty and undignified exit.

21

'I'm sorry, but there's somewhere else I need to go,' Julia told Jake when she got back to the car. 'It looks like there will be no walk with Leo today after all.'

WALK! – his favourite word. Jake whined in delight and turned his large body in circles – no mean feat in the back seat of a small car. He banged the back of Julia's seat, and his tail whipped against the windows. The whole car trembled.

'No, I said *not* going for a...'

Julia stopped herself just in time, realising her mistake. Jake's vocabulary was limited, and he was selectively deaf when it suited him, but 'walk' was one word he never missed. The word 'no' and its close relative 'not' were words that seemed unrecognisable to his doggy brain.

'Okay, Jakey, calm down.' She stroked his ears, which some-times worked to settle him. 'Sit down. I'll tell you what, I'll drop you home first. You can hang out with Henny Penny and Chaplin while I go and see Hayley.'

Jake was, frankly, bored with her itinerary and with her commentary. There had been all too much driving, waiting and talking, and too little snacking and walking, as far as he was concerned. When Julia started the car, he gazed wistfully out of the window.

Once home, Jake leapt from the car as if he was being released from prison. Even Chaplin seemed annoyed at their long absence. He was sitting on the front doormat glaring at them like a stern father waiting for a tardy teenager who had missed her curfew. Julia half expected him to tap his wristwatch and demand to know exactly what time she thought it was, young lady.

Julia dashed to the back garden to let the chickens out, and saw that Henny 'Houdini' Penny had let herself out already. Jake galloped up to her and snuffled her chestnut feathers with his big brown nose. 'Right then, you behave yourselves, I'm off,' Julia said, having checked the water bowls and general state of things. 'If it's quick, we might still be able to...' She stopped herself just in time, and said, 'Ambulate.'

As she got back into the car, she had a bit of a laugh at her own joke, but sobered up rather quickly at the thought of going to see Hayley. She'd been warned about coming with another of what the detective liked to call her 'half-baked ideas and improbable theories'. And the more she thought about it, the more she realised that this one was based on an assumption – that the 'Bethie' in the phone conversation was Bethany. Julia couldn't see who else it could possibly be, but that was the sort of detail that Hayley liked to home in on, and then she would give Julia one of her looks, or worse, one of her talks about minding her own business. The theory was based on *two* unproven premises, in fact – the other being that Roger Grave and Bethany had something going on between them. Julia had no evidence of either fact. And without that, 'half-baked ideas and improbable theories' rather accurately covered the situation.

One thing about Julia Bird, though: she wasn't long out of ideas.

Julia seldom shopped at the supermarket that Graham had managed and where Bethany worked. It was on the very edge of Berrywick, on the opposite side from Julia's house. It wasn't more than a five-minute drive, but Julia was in the habit of shopping at the little shops in the high street. She was usually only shopping for one – one human, that was – and more often than not, she picked up two or three items on her walks, or on her way to Second Chances or the Buttered Scone. She enjoyed the ease and neighbourliness of it, and only went to a bigger shop, by car, once a month or so.

The shop wasn't busy. It was 2.30 p.m., after the lunchtime shoppers, and before the rush of people stopping on the way home from fetching children or from work. Bethany was easy to spot, thanks to her red hair, which she wore pulled up in a tight, no-nonsense ponytail. She was in the cleaning products aisle with a clipboard and a pen, presumably doing some sort of stock-related activity. It would be a big job. The sheer number of cleaning products in the world was one of the things that made Julia feel like some peasant transported from the nineteenth century. She was ninety-eight per cent convinced that there were only three distinct products, and the rest was packaging and smells. Furthermore, she felt sure that water, bleach and vinegar would take care of household hygiene. But she could never entirely resist the pressure to buy floor cleaner, tile cleaner, oven cleaner, window cleaner...

'Oh hello, it's you!' Julia said to Bethany, in what she hoped sounded like surprise. 'I'm Julia, we met at the funeral.'

She added this, knowing that young people didn't seem to be able to remember and recognise older people. She imagined they thought they all looked the same. It was part of the invisibility of old age.

'Of course I remember you, Julia,' said Bethany. 'You were very kind. You gave me tissues and sweets.'

'How are you doing? It must be hard being back at work without Graham.'

'Oh, it's sad and weird, but when you're busy, it takes your mind off things for a bit.'

'Well, I hope you've got good support.'

'Not really...'

'And you've got Roger Grave to lean on, haven't you?' Julia hoped that she was not being too direct.

Bethany looked at her in mild surprise. 'Oh, do you know him?'

'I do, actually.'

'And how did you work out we were...?'

'I'm a social worker; I have a bit of an instinct for human relationships. I put two and two together.'

'Well, I mean, quite a few people know by now; it's not the secret it once was. So I suppose there's not a lot of putting together needed, really.'

Times really had changed. Grave was a senior policeman, and old enough to be Bethany's father, and if what Bethany said was true, it was an open secret that the two of them were involved in a relationship, and no one batted an eyelid.

'Anyway, it's not as if he's very supportive as far as Graham is concerned,' Bethany said.

'Graham?' Julia wasn't sure if the young woman would be pleased to realise that Julia knew about the affair.

Bethany dropped her voice. 'Graham was in love with me,' she said. 'He was going to leave Jane.'

'You can see why Roger might not have liked that.' Julia felt she was rather understating the situation.

'I suppose he's very protective, and he didn't think the relationship with Graham was good for me.'

'I can imagine it's been quite difficult for you, being torn between the two of them.'

'That's exactly it! It's as if they think they were in some sort of competition for my attention.'

'Understandable, really, when you think of it. Two men, both of whom care for you.' Julia was slightly stunned by how openly Bethany was talking about this, but told herself again that times had changed.

Bethany was still speaking. 'Exactly, and you know what dads are like with their daughters.'

Dads? Why was she talking about dads now? Not that she could blame Bethany's dad, whoever he was, for being worried for his daughter. This wasn't the kind of arrangement a parent dreamed of for their child.

Bethany glanced around the shop to make sure no one was in earshot, and went on: 'Of course, with Graham being married, Dad was not at all happy. But like I said to him, "It's not like you've got much of a leg to stand on, Regional Superintendent Grave. Mum was actually engaged to someone else when she fell pregnant with me."'

Wait. What?

Roger Grave was Bethany's *dad*? Julia was struck dumb. She actually did not know what to say at this surprise revelation. This passed unnoticed, because Bethany was more than prepared to keep up the conversation on her side. 'I feel like I can talk to you, Julia. I've got no one to talk to about this, really. All the other girls here disapprove – they think I'm awful for getting involved with a married man, and my boss at that. My mum doesn't even know about it; she would be very upset and disapproving, too. I mean, I don't blame her, I feel bad about it. Bad about his wife. I know it was wrong. It wasn't the plan at all, but we were spending all this time together at work, and next thing we knew, Graham and I were in love.'

Bethany looked so sad and wistful that Julia couldn't help but feel sorry for her. She was a young woman who, for the sake of love, had done something she knew was morally suspect, and now she'd lost everything.

'I told Dad we were in love, that Graham's marriage was over and we were going to be together. Of course, he was furious. He blamed Graham. He thought he had taken advantage of me. And he'd already cast him in the play when he found out about us, which made it even more awkward. I was worried there would be trouble between them in the production, but apparently they mostly kept it professional. Although he did have a chat with Graham, made it clear that if he was serious about me, he needed to leave his wife. And that helped a lot.'

'Bethany, did your father ever threaten Graham?'

'No, of course not! I mean, not seriously. He did tell me he'd like to punch him in the face. But you know my dad. He's all talk. He would never *hurt* him.'

'You're sure?'

Bethany's voice rose alarmingly. 'Of course I'm sure! Oh, my God, Julia! You can't think he had anything to do with the shooting. That was an accident! And besides, Dad is a policeman! He would never dream of doing such a thing.'

Julia was considering how best to ask Bethany about the conversation she'd overheard, when the younger woman said, 'Oh-oh, here comes trouble.'

Julia followed her gaze, and saw a bossy-looking woman marching towards them.

'The assistant manager. She has designs on Graham's job, and of course she doesn't like me. I'd better get back to work,' Bethany whispered, before saying, at normal volume: 'Here you are, then. These are the floor polishes. All sorts, we have, and a number of different sizes. Sprays, of course, and, um, wax, and this one smells of lavender and that one's lemon...'

'Thanks for your help. You've been very informative,' said Julia, grabbing the nearest can of something from the shelf. As she swept past the assistant manager, who was now bearing down the aisle like a small brunette tank, Julia repeated herself loudly, for good measure: 'Very helpful and informative indeed, thank you, Bethany.'

22

Hayley Gibson listened to Julia's story with a look of brooding irritation, her arms crossed over her chest, and an eyebrow raising occasionally in what Julia took to be disbelief. But once she'd talked her way into the DI's office, and got her attention, Julia was determined to tell her everything, succinctly, but in full.

When Julia mentioned Bethany's affair with Graham, Hayley looked as if she might explode. 'Damn it! I knew Jane was holding something back. When she finally admitted that they were headed towards divorce, she didn't mention the affair. When I asked her about the reasons, she just said, "Oh, you know... we drifted apart." I think she even used the word "amicable".'

'According to Hannah, once Graham was dead, Jane decided to just pretend the separation never happened to protect his reputation – and hers, I suppose,' Julia said. 'How she thought she'd make that work I don't know. It was bound to come up somehow. You can't keep a secret like that forever, not with an investigation into an unnatural death.'

'Well, you dug it up.' Hayley spoke with grudging admiration.

'And there's more,' said Julia.

When she got to the revelation about Roger Grave being Bethany's father, Hayley reacted: 'Her *father*? Are you kidding me? How did I not know *that*?'

'Well, you weren't even talking to Bethany. She wasn't involved in the play. And Roger wasn't a suspect, so it's not as if you were looking at his personal life.' Julia ended with a disclaimer: 'I am not trying to interfere, Hayley. I'm just telling you what I've discovered. Roger Grave did have a motive – Graham Powell was having an affair with his daughter – and he had opportunity, given where the murder took place. I could be adding one and one and making three – that's for you to decide – but either way, this situation between Graham, Roger and Bethany is complicated and fraught, and probably worth investigating.'

'Okay.'

'What?'

'Okay, I hear you.' Hayley was reaching for her phone. 'I find it very hard to imagine Grave had anything to do with Graham's death, but there does seem to be something off in this connection. Something between the three of them. I'm phoning him now.'

Julia waited, hearing the faint tinny ringing tone coming from Hayley's phone. There was a knock on the door. It opened a crack and a head appeared. A familiar head – male, youngish, straggly dark hair and rather a pleasant face wearing a tentative expression – but Julia couldn't quite place it.

'Another delivery for DI Gibson. The reception lady said I could bring this through,' he said.

Hayley, phone still to her ear, nodded, and he stepped into her office.

'Brian?' Julia's voice was pure astonishment.

It was the same young man who had delivered Oscar's flowers to Julia the previous week, the one who Julia had embarrassingly mistaken for Hayley's date. Blushing at the memory of her crazy assumption, Julia noticed that Hayley was a similar shade of pink, presumably on account of the admirer who was sending what appeared to be a very nice basket of fruit, chocolates and other treats.

Brian, wearing the same black jeans and black leather jacket as last time, was the only one not flushed with embarrassment. He gazed around, looking for a place to set the basket down. It was a hopeless search.

'I'll take it,' said Julia, reaching for it. 'Thank you.'

Brian handed it over with relief and beat a hasty retreat.

Now, Julia was left with the problem of finding a clear space amongst the drifts and slopes of Hayley's paperwork. There was no such thing, so she put it on the floor in the corner, noting the lovely selection – a slab of macadamia nut brittle looked particularly tempting. There was a note card attached, which, sadly, Julia was not able to read at this distance. Who, she wondered, was the generous soul behind the gift? And why had they sent it? Was it Hayley's birthday? No, that was definitely early in the year. She noticed the brilliant white orchid that she'd seen on her last visit to Hayley. That had been a gift, too, that Cherise had mentioned. Was it from the same person? Did Hayley Gibson have an admirer?

Hayley, meanwhile, had made another call and was speaking: 'What time was the meeting? Right. Yes, I know, he's very punctual... Yes, I tried his mobile too... Well, when he comes in, will you ask him to phone me? Thank you.'

Hayley ended the call and squinted into the middle distance, as she tended to do when deeply considering a problem.

'Well, I suppose I should be on my way,' Julia said. 'Enjoy your goody basket, Hayley.'

Julia had hoped to perhaps prompt some explanation as to the basket's provenance, but Hayley looked at it as if she'd forgotten it was there, and said, 'Thanks.'

'It looks delicious.'

'It does.'

Julia could contain herself no longer: 'Hayley, do you have an admirer? A beau?'

Hayley wore the funny, squiffy expression of someone trying to suppress a smile. 'Yes, Julia, I do indeed.'

Julia waited expectantly, an encouraging smile on her own face, but no further information was forthcoming. In fact, a frown appeared on Hayley's forehead. 'I need to speak to Roger Grave urgently.'

Julia hoped she wasn't sending the detective on a wild goose chase.

'Jane Powell – the victim's widow – is being detained for questioning, on my orders. If there's another narrative, another theory, I need to hear it. If there's another suspect, I need to get that poor woman out of there. And for that, I need to see Roger Grave. His input could be key to solving this case. And he's chosen this very day to disappear. He didn't go to work. He missed a meeting. And he's not answering his phone. Very unusual behaviour.'

'That is odd, isn't it?' said Julia. 'From my experience of him at the theatre, he's utterly punctual and reliable.'

'Likewise, at work. I'm concerned,' said Hayley. 'I'm going to swing by his house and see if he's there.'

'Now?'

'Yes.' Hayley was on her feet now, shoving first one arm and then the other into her coat. She took a step towards the door, grabbing her handbag as she went. 'Damn.' She stopped short.

'What is it?'

'My car is in the garage. They're fixing the brakes. Again. I'll have to phone Walter Farmer, see if there's a car available.'

'I can give you a lift. My car's right outside. It's no trouble, the drive is only ten minutes or so. I'll tell Wilma I will be at the shop a bit later than I thought. They'll manage fine without me.'

Hayley appeared to be weighing up her options. Her conundrum was clear – she didn't want Julia tagging along on police business, but getting a lift from her would be the simplest and quickest solution to her transport problem.

'Okay, thanks,' she said, quite ungraciously. 'I want to see if Roger's home, and if he's okay, and then question him.'

Julia hadn't thought, when she had initiated this whole situation, that she would be present when it played out. Now she felt rather nervous. Grave, in his Regional Superintendent persona, was quite scary – and here she was, implying he might be involved in a murder. 'Well, they're not really theories, more like... I suppose, observations...'

'Let's go.'

Hayley was a brisk walker, and Julia had to trot to catch her up.

'Going out,' Hayley barked at Cherise. 'An hour or so, I expect.'

Cherise appeared not to notice Hayley's brusque manner and purposeful stride. She started gushing delightedly, 'Gosh, another delivery for you, boss! And wasn't it lovely? Goodness, whoever is sending these lovely gifts deserves a chance, I'd say. If you're not interested, you can send him my way. A fellow like that would be...'

Hayley made as if she didn't hear a word emanating from the front desk, and strode through the door, Julia scurrying after her.

Roger Grave's house was on the outskirts of the neighbouring village of Edgeley. Hayley had been there for a drinks party the previous Christmas, not long after Roger Grave had moved there, and knew where to go. Julia followed her directions as obediently and confidently as she would the Google Maps lady whose plummy tones instructed her on her way around the Cotswolds.

'Left here... Straight over at the roundabout... Turn right by the school...'

In between directions, there was mostly silence, both women mulling over things in their heads.

'Here we are. You can pull over here.' Hayley gestured to a small stone house set just back from the road, with a neat, if not treasured, garden along the front side.

Hayley's hand was on the door handle before Julia's little red Fiat had come to a complete stop.

'Come on then, let's see what's up with Roger.'

Julia got out and locked the car. This was a London habit that she'd never managed to shake, despite the continued ribbing of her fellow villagers – 'What do you think, it's going to be *stolen*?' followed by guffaws of laughter. She followed Hayley to the front door with a prickly sense of foreboding. She wondered about Roger's personal life. He had never mentioned a wife, and she'd assumed him to be single. Clearly, given the Bethany discovery, any assumptions she might have about his life meant nothing, but in this case she had been correct.

'He lives alone,' said Hayley, 'so if he's not here, we're on a wasted mission.'

She knocked on the green-painted front door.

No answer.

She knocked again, wearily this time, as if she knew it would be in vain.

This time, her knock got a response. A high-pitched yapping bark from inside the house. The barks got louder, closer, until the dog was on the other side of the front door. It jumped at the door – Julia worried for the woodwork on the other side, as she heard the little thing hurl itself halfway up the door and then scrape its nails on the way down. On the fourth jump, the dog's foot must have snagged the door handle and its weight pulled it down. The door cracked open to reveal a bouncy golden spaniel, going berserk.

'It's okay, boy, we're just visiting your dad, Roger,' Julia said, bending down to calm him. 'Everything's all right.'

Except it wasn't. Everything wasn't all right at all.

The door creaked open wider to reveal – there on the floor by the front door, beside the neat row of wellies and running shoes – the splayed, lifeless body of Superintendent Roger Grave.

23

'*The Complete Works of William Shakespeare?*' said DC Walter Farmer, gently lifting the front cover of the weighty hardcover tome with a clean handkerchief. 'What's that all about?'

Bob Jones, the new forensics chap, scratched his big head with short, blunt fingers and sighed a deep, thoughtful sigh. 'Well, it's about life, innit? Love, death, betrayal, misunderstandings... The whole sorry mess. You name it, it's all in that there book. There's the thirty-seven plays just for starters – you've got your comedies, your tragedies, your historical plays...'

Walter Farmer stared in utter bewilderment as the man counted them out on his stubby fingers, bending each finger back as he enumerated the types of Shakespearean plays. Julia was likewise surprised at the turn the forensic investigation had taken. Bob's predecessor at the forensic unit hadn't been much for talking, and when he had talked, it hadn't been about Shakespeare, that was for sure.

Bob continued, unfazed, 'And that's before you even get to the sonnets. My favourites, if I must be honest. They're mostly about love, of course. But also beauty, and, like, the passing of

160   KATIE GAYLE

time, y'know? And mortality... It's all there. I mean, that's life
for you, innit?'

He looked down at Farmer, who was still squatting at Roger
Grave's feet, next to the big book, hankie in hand. Farmer, realising he was expecting an answer, nodded.

'So to answer your question, I'd say this book is about life,
really. Life in all its complexity.'

Walter stood up to frown at the man in confusion. 'I meant,
what's it all about, in terms of the crime? Why is the book here?
Who dropped it? What's it got to do with Superintendent
Grave's death?'

'Oh, that! Ah, well, yes, my mistake. I don't know for sure,
but it could be that the superintendent was whacked on the
head with this here book. It's a tragedy, really.'

Was that a *joke*? A Shakespeare joke at the side of the dead
body of a senior policeman? Surely not. Looking at Bob, Julia
couldn't say for sure. For all his literary observations, he had the
lumpy, impassive face of a retired boxer. If it was a joke, Walter
Farmer certainly didn't get it. He looked as blank as, well, a
blank page.

'Looks to me like he fell and hit his head on the hall table,'
Walter said, moving on from Shakespeare to more concrete
matters. They all looked at the antique wooden table next to
Roger Grave's head. It was narrow, the perfect table for the
space, but solidly built. A dark smudge on the corner seemed to
bear out Walter's theory.

'My working guess is that it happened last night. Looks to
me like he was whacked with the bard's *Works* before he fell
and hit his head on the table,' Bob Jones countered, standing up
tall, his hands on his hips. Forensics chaps liked to show up the
working coppers when they could, so there was a hint of self-
satisfaction about his answer, but he kept a smile on his face to
show there were no hard feelings.

Seeing as Hayley Gibson was outside with the other guy from the forensic team, Julia decided to venture a question.

'What makes you say that?'

'Well, it's early days and I'm not a clairvoyant,' Bob said, modestly, as if he was, in fact, such a thing, but didn't like to boast, 'but it seems to me that bruise on the victim's head is the same shape as the corner of that there book. And the corner of that there book is a bit flattened, see?'

Walter and Julia peered at it. It did seem so.

'The book's in good nick. You can see it's been well looked-after. Look inside – it's full of notes. Someone treasures this book. That flattened piece is new, is my feeling. So it seems to me – and like I said, I can't be sure, not without the lab results – it seems to me that Superintendent Grave was hit on the head with the *Complete Works*, either tripped or collapsed to the floor, and died from hitting his head on the table. You'd be amazed how often it happens, to be honest.'

Julia could only assume that this was a reference to the table, and not to the blow from *The Complete Works of Shakespeare*. She didn't imagine that *that* happened often at all. She looked down at Roger's body, his long legs splayed at an odd angle, one arm reaching over his head, and the other trapped uncomfortably beneath him. Blood had seeped from under his head – from a wound or his ear, she couldn't tell – and pooled on the wooden floor. He was a good-looking man in a stiff, angular sort of way, and he remained so in death. His colour, though was pale and greyish, and beginning to show the mottle of the recently deceased. Julia felt suddenly queasy, and moved to the front door. Outside, she leaned over and put her hands on her knees, taking a few deep breaths to calm herself and ease her sickly feeling.

Hayley Gibson came up behind her and asked, briskly, 'You all right?'

'Yes. Just... shocked, I suppose.'

'Well, it's shocking, that's for sure. Listen, you go home. Roger Grave is a top policeman. His death is bringing out the big guns. And the big brass. And the big... everything. They'll be all over this crime scene like a rash before the hour is up. Walter has taken your statement; we know where to find you for follow-up information.'

'Yes, yes, I think I'll go. But before I do, Hayley, there's something I need to tell you...'

Hayley's clever blue eyes were on Julia in a flash. 'What is it?'

'It's about Bethany.'

'Yes?'

'Do you think she might have... Is she a suspect?'

'I know you like the girl, but I'm sorry to say, she's definitely got quite some explaining to do. If she thought her father was involved in her lover's murder, then she would have had reason to confront him, perhaps even hit him with the book – although it looks as if it might have been the fall onto that table that killed him.'

'That's just it. I asked her about it. I asked if it was possible that Roger Grave might have threatened Graham, or hurt him. She was shocked, and completely denied he would ever do anything violent.'

'Well, if she didn't believe her father killed Graham Powell, then she wouldn't have any reason to confront him.'

'Unless I inadvertently convinced her that he might be involved. The thing is, Hayley, she was *genuinely* astonished at the idea. She honestly hadn't even considered the possibility. I was the one who put the idea in her head. If Bethany killed her father, it's because I prompted her to do it.'

Hayley was having none of this. 'Unless you smacked Roger Grave on the head yourself, you're not to blame for his death, no matter what you said to Bethany. If it was Bethany, then that's on her. Don't worry yourself about that, Julia. Let me and the rest of the force do our job.'

'You'll speak to her, then?'

'Of course. Already in process. DC Farmer is going to go and break the news and ask her to come in. We'll bring her in and see what she has to say. I'll meet him at the station when I'm done here. As of now, Bethany is on the top of the list of people to interview.'

'As a suspect?'

'Julia, this investigation is in the very early stages. And besides, you know I can't give you information about individuals.'

'Okay, yes, of course, I understand. And what about Jane?'

'I've already given instructions for her to be released. Grave's death makes her involvement in her husband's death look less likely. I find it hard to believe that the two murders are not connected, and Jane was locked up when Grave was killed. Even if she did cover up her marital troubles.'

This, at least, was good news. Julia had hated the idea of Jane being in jail overnight again.

'Julia, don't mention the book to anyone. It's the kind of detail we don't release, okay?'

'No problem, I understand.'

'Go on. You go home. There's nothing for you to do here, and you still look terribly pale.'

Julia remembered that she'd driven Hayley to Roger's house. She didn't have a car there. 'Will you be okay for a lift?'

'Believe me, Julia, half the cop cars in the Cotswolds are on their way here. I'll be fine for a lift. Now go.'

'Okay. Bye, Hayley. Good luck.'

Julia drove home slowly, trying to absorb the latest turn of events. Nothing felt quite real, and she was relieved to let herself into her home, greet her beloved Jake, and put the kettle on. As soon as she had a cup of tea in her hand, she gave Sean a call.

'Perfect timing, you clever thing,' he said as he answered the phone. 'I'm right between patients.'

'Oh, Sean. You won't believe what's happened.'

'Well, as long as no one died, that's the main thing.'

'Well...' She took a gulp of her tea to find she had completely over-sweetened it. It just showed what a state she was in. There was a long silence while she swallowed the unpalatable mouthful and tried to think of a delicate way of phrasing what had happened.

Sean spoke first. 'What? You can't be serious. Someone died? Who?'

'Roger Grave.'

'The superintendent? When? How?'

'Sometime last night. It's not entirely clear how, but it definitely wasn't natural causes.'

'And were you...?'

Julia felt fragile, and not up to repeating the whole grisly story over the phone. 'Sean, can you come over? I could use the company. I'll tell you everything when I see you.'

'Of course.' He didn't hesitate. 'I have a couple more patients, and I'll have to pop home to feed Leo first.'

'There's no rush. Why don't you come for supper? You can bring Leo. And Jono, of course. They're both very welcome.'

'If you're sure?'

'Absolutely sure.'

'Well, let me bring the supper. I can stop at the new curry place we've been wanting to try, and pick up a takeaway.'

'Oh, well, that's a kind offer. But I can just make a bowl of pasta. I've got a jar of pesto in the fridge, it's no trouble...' It wasn't much trouble, but she wasn't exactly in the mood for even simple food preparation. She dropped her half-hearted protests, and said, 'Actually, I don't feel like cooking and I would love a curry. Thank you.'

'Ah, now that wasn't too hard, was it?' She could hear him smiling as he spoke. 'It sounds like you've had enough for today. It's decided. I'll see you around six thirty with something delicious and comforting. It's my turn to look after you.'

24

With nothing to do but dwell on Roger's death and wait for Sean, Julia decided that she might as well get Jake – and herself – out for a short walk before the light fell. The long summer evenings were over. It was starting to get dark earlier, and chilly, too. She would need to get a move on. She fetched Jake's lead from the hook by the front door.

Jake could hear the merest clink of his lead from miles away. Astonishingly enough, this was the case even when he was, ostensibly, asleep. Before Julia had a chance to call his name he was inside and at her feet, bounding and barking. Henny Penny was looking ruffled and disgruntled in the spot where they'd been lying.

'All right, Jakey. Good boy. Settle down,' she muttered soothingly, to absolutely no effect. The only thing that calmed him was getting out into the road, and starting the walk. Once they were on their way, he would downgrade his state quite quickly from 'hysterical' to 'overexcited' and eventually – after about ten minutes – to simply 'having a good time'. Julia ushered him out of the door, clipped on the lead and started walking. He was still in the 'overexcited' state when Aunt Edna appeared on the path, coming towards them.

'Good afternoon, Aunt Edna. You're looking well.'

'Well' might be something of an overstatement, but it was true that Aunt Edna seemed to have reached a sort of equilibrium. She was so ancient that she never seemed to get any older. She remained reed thin, tottery on her feet, confusing in her communication, yet, somehow, oddly unchanged. One could not discount the possibility of immortality.

'All's well that ends well,' said Edna in a sing-song voice, and then enquired of Jake, 'Don't you think so, young man? All's well, except for bad boys...'

Jake was terrified of the old woman, although in truth she had more to fear from a solid hunk of Labrador than he had to fear from her. One good wag of his tail would knock her off her feet, and from there, a broken hip would be a dead cert, by the look of her frail bones. Jake looked up at Julia for help, the whites of his eyes showing.

'And except for murder most foul,' Edna continued cheerfully. 'Not well at all. Beginning or ending.' She wagged her finger at Julia and repeated the words, 'Murder most foul.'

Aunt Edna took hold of the end of a purple scarf – one of many in which she was entangled – and flung it dramatically round her neck. She doffed her non-existent hat in their direction, wished them both, 'Good evening,' and wobbled off.

Jake sighed in relief when they walked on.

'I wonder what she meant by that. "Murder most foul". She says the oddest things, does Edna, although some of the odd things are odd in a sort of meaningful way, aren't they? I mean, there has just been a murder. Two. And it is certainly most foul. And if I'm not mistaken, that's a quote from Shakespeare. Is it *Hamlet*?'

She didn't expect an answer from the dog, which she took to mean that talking to him in the first place wasn't a sign of encroaching senility on her own part. It was expecting answers that got you put away for your own protection.

She took Jake for a good long walk, greeting familiar faces and even more familiar dogs as she went. She could never decide if she loved this part of village life or not – the endless meetings and greetings meant she couldn't just take a quiet walk and have a good think. The one thing that her mind kept circling back to was Roger's death, and the things she had learnt about his life just before he died. Would it all tie up, she wondered? Heading towards home, yet another familiar figure came into view. This one was male and gangly, and sitting broodily on a bench overlooking the river. He was eating a sandwich, tossing bits of crust to the ducks between bites. It was DC Walter Farmer.

Julia had decided not to interrupt his deep thoughts, and simply to walk on by, when he seemed to snap out of whatever it was he was thinking. He turned towards Jake, and greeted him with a click of the tongue. Jake stopped and rested his big head on Walter's thigh, taking the opportunity to snuffle up a few breadcrumbs while he was about it. Walter stroked his ears and sighed.

'Long day, I imagine,' Julia said, sympathetically. She noticed that his face, which at the best of times was pale and sported a few lingering teenage spots, was afflicted with an uncomfortable-looking rash, which she put down to stress.

'Very long, and it's not over. I just came out here for a bit of a breather. We'll be working a good few hours yet, me and the boss.'

'You'll be tired.'

'It's not just the long hours. It's the responsibility, you know. Roger Grave, he was one of us. He was in our village. And now he's dead. On our watch.'

Julia hadn't thought of it quite like that. She felt for Walter, and for Hayley Gibson, too. Before she could offer words of sympathy, Walter continued. 'It's a terrible, terrible situation. And we've got nothing to work with.'

'Do you know any more about what happened?' she asked. 'Are the forensics back?'

'Not yet.'

'I'm sure they're prioritising the forensics, Grave being a policeman.'

'Oh yes, they are. And you know, if a policeman is killed, we immediately consider what cases he's working on. So there's a lot of coppers working on that. See if there's anyone with a grudge, or anyone who might want to silence him.'

Julia hadn't considered the possibility that Roger's death might be completely unrelated to Graham's. That it might have nothing to do with Bethany, and the complicated personal relationships at play in Berrywick. That he might have been involved in investigating a drug cartel, or some such. Although frankly, she couldn't imagine that a drug cartel would use *The Complete Works of Shakespeare* and an antique hall table as their weapons of choice.

Walter continued, 'I'm working the other angle. And our prime interview subject, the one person we thought might know something, was beyond useless.'

'You mean Bethany?'

'Yes. She claims she's made a big night of it. Drowning her sorrows, you know. Claims she can barely remember a thing – what time she went where, who she saw, who might have seen her.'

'Well, that seems rather convenient.'

'Doesn't it just? And the other thing is, we have to be careful with her. She's a grieving daughter, too, and we need to be sensitive. We've asked her a few questions, but we can't just be dragging her in for a tough session with DI Gibson.' There was a pause and Walter gave a tiny, almost imperceptible shudder at the idea of it. 'Anyway, so now I'm tracking down her movements to see if she can be accounted for all that time. I'm on my way to the various pubs, trying to find people who might remember seeing her, to see if I can connect the timeline. I just thought I'd have five minutes of peace and quiet to watch the ducks and eat my sandwich before I set off. It's the first time I've had a minute.'

The half-eaten sandwich was still in his hand, wrapped in wax paper, cheese and tomato showing through the bite marks. It looked home-made, and Julia wondered if he'd made it himself, or his young wife had. Either way, it was a sweetly domestic thing to see, a sandwich from home. Walter looked at it, sighed, pushed the paper back, and took a large bite.

'Good luck with the investigation, Walter. I hope you find answers very soon. And I hope, I really hope, it's not Bethany who killed Roger Grave.'

That last sentence just slipped out, sadly. It felt unbearable, the idea of a child killing a parent. Almost as awful as a parent killing a child.

Walter brought the remains of the sandwich to his mouth and was about to bite into it when he changed his mind. He tore it in two, and tossed one piece to the ducks still bobbing hopefully in the river in front of them, and the other half to Jake, who snapped it out of the air with so much concentration and precision that he might have been competing in some Olympic sport.

'I hope so too, Mrs Bird. I hope so too.'

25

A warm, fragrant fug filled the kitchen when Sean opened the packet. There was cinnamon, for sure, and cardamom. Cumin. Ginger. Was that the liquorice smell of star anise that Julia was picking up?

Sean placed three large tubs on the kitchen table.

'There's a lamb vindaloo – I ordered that one extra hot – a milder chicken and cashew nut curry, a spicy dhal, a dozen cheese samosas, some onion bhaji and a chicken biryani,' he said, taking various containers out of the bag. 'And then there's rice times three. And here's naan bread, and then some condiments.'

'It smells divine, and it looks like enough for an army!'

Sean and Jono exchanged wry smiles, and the younger man said, 'That would be me. I'm the army.'

'He's feeding himself up,' said Sean. 'Building a bit of muscle.'

'Making music isn't exactly the healthiest lifestyle. I've got a bit scrawny and out of shape. But I'm making an effort to eat better while I'm with Dad. I even went for a run.'

'Leo approves wholeheartedly of this new regime, as you can imagine.'

'I'm sure he does! You'd like that, wouldn't you, Jakey? Extra runs. Extra snacks. Now, who wants what to drink?'

Sean fixed the drinks while Julia started setting the table.

'You're in a good place for running,' Julia said. She gave Jono a handful of knives and forks to put out, and opened the cupboard for the plates. 'We've got lots of lovely routes. We walk a lot of them, of course, with the dogs. You can go through the woods and over to the big lake – it's a bit cold now, but it's lovely for a swim in the summer.'

'There are quite a few winter swimmers,' said Sean, putting a glass of wine in front of Julia's place at the head of the table, and an apple juice in front of Jono. He didn't ask either of them what they wanted. 'It's taken off, that cold swimming. Absolute lunacy if you ask me, but there seems to be some evidence it's good for you. It's not for me, but you might like it.'

'I think I'll stick with the running for now, thanks, Dad. It's enough of a shock to the system.'

Julia put the plates down on the placemats. 'Well, the river's my favourite route. It's lovely with the ducks, and the little boats. Jake and I were there earlier this evening, weren't we, Jakey?'

Jake and Leo were disinterested in the conversation, both pooped after their walk and run respectively. They were lying side by side under the kitchen table, which would be mildly awkward for the diners' feet, but they'd work around it.

'I saw the river at sunset last night,' Jono said. 'So beautiful. I was at the Swan for supper.'

'With Laine,' said Sean, raising his eyebrows at Julia.

Ah, a date with Laine, she thought. She wondered if anything had happened between the two of them, but didn't like to pry. She didn't want to be too nosy about the date, and make him feel pressurised. Instead, she asked a more neutral warm-up question: 'How was it? I haven't eaten there in a while.'

'The food was good. We went to the pub, not to the fancier restaurant. There are some tables a bit away from the bar, where it's quiet. We had burgers. Laine is vegetarian, so hers was a veg burger. She said it was good, too.'

Julia played it cool. 'She seems nice, Laine. In the brief time we met her. And I did like her goat. And it's not every day you see a goat walking on a lead.'

'Gruff. That's the goat's name.'

'From the "Three Billy Goats Gruff", I presume?' Sean asked.

'Yes, except she's a nanny goat, so it doesn't make much sense.'

'Still. It's a cute name. Shall we eat? Help yourselves.'

They filled their plates straight from the tubs, scooping the rich sauces over piles of rice.

'I'm glad to hear the food at the Swan was nice,' said Julia. 'I haven't been in ages. My ex-husband got married there last year, and I haven't been back since.'

'Oh, I'm so sorry,' Jono looked horribly flustered. 'That must have been, um... Gosh, how sad for you. Or, I mean, awkward...'

'Oh no, I didn't mind about his marriage. In fact, I think it's a good thing!'

'Well, that's, I mean... that's good. Um, and she's nice, is she?'

'Who?'

'His wife. The new one.'

'There's no wife. He married Christopher. A man.'

'Of course, well. That's good. I mean. If he's nice. The husband. I mean. Your husband's husband. Ex-husband's husband. Christopher.' Jono blushed scarlet. 'I'm sorry, I'm making a right mess of things, aren't I?'

Sean looked from one to the other with a pained expression.

Julia was calm, in fact slightly amused, and tried her best to put Jono out of his misery. 'Not at all, Jono! You weren't to know. It's all very amicable. I'm happy that Peter's happy. Christopher is a lovely man. I am pleased they are married. Jess, our daughter, is fine with it all. That is not why I haven't gone back to the Swan.'

'Ah, well, that's good,' said Jono, turning his attention most diligently to the vindaloo. The scarlet drained slowly from his face as he cut into the succulent lamb.

Sean caught Julia's eye and smiled a wry smile. What they hadn't told the young man was that the fact that Julia's ex-husband had been one of the grooms had not been the most traumatic part of the wedding at the Swan. No, that would have to have been the frozen body they had discovered the next morning. Of course, there had also been a dramatic allergy attack, as a distant second in the trauma stakes. But neither of them mentioned either of those events.

After a few forkfuls of curry, Jono had composed himself enough to continue. 'Well, I hope Peter and Christopher had a DJ, or at least a playlist on an iPhone, instead of what we had, which was a very drunk red-headed girl playing awful love songs on the jukebox, and singing along.' He did a little thing on an invisible guitar and crooned, 'I-yyye-I will aaaaalways love you...'

'Poor thing. Maybe she had a heartbreak,' Sean said. 'Maybe she had just broken up with her boyfriend and was drowning her sorrows and listening to maudlin music.' Sean looked pleased with his invented history.

'Not a break-up,' said Jono. 'Someone died, apparently. Laine recognised her; she'd been a few years above Laine at school. We'd finished eating and moved to the bar counter for a coffee. The girl was telling Laine a long, sad story, but I didn't listen in too closely. It seemed rude, when the girl was spilling her heart out. A married man, I got the impression. Then a death. Possibly a murder. It was all very complicated.'

It sounded very much, thought Julia with some surprise, like Jono had seen Bethany at the Swan.

'And then, as well as her, some other fella came in and sat on the other side of me. He downed three shots of tequila in a row. Believe me, this was not a guy who could hold his drink. Soon he was telling anyone who'd listen about his acting career. He'd been in that TV programme about the newspaper barons. Remember it, Dad? Mum used to watch it.' Julia felt an odd little jolt at the mention of Sean's wife, Jono's mother, who had died of cancer some years before Julia had met Sean. He had told Julia about his wife and her death, but it wasn't something they talked about often. And she'd never heard her referred to as 'Mum'. It made her sad. Jono had been in his teens when he'd lost his mother. No wonder he'd had a hard time finding his feet. He was grieving.

'*Hot Press*, it was called,' Sean said. 'Full of very well turned-out journalists, evil press owners, secret sources. It's a wonder they had time to get the paper out, what with all the steamy affairs. I used to tease your mum mercilessly about it, but she loved that programme. Said it was relaxing after a long day. Didn't demand an ounce of brainpower.'

It couldn't have been anyone but Hector yammering on about *Hot Press*. Berrywick was a small village, but still – what were the chances?

'Right, well, he starred in that, apparently,' Jono continued. 'So he was bending my ear. And this drunk girl – Brittany, her name was – was bending Laine's ear, and the date took rather a turn for the worse. Made me glad I'd given up drinking, though, I can tell you. We took Brittany home in the end. Laine had her dad's car. She doesn't drink either. So we drove the girl home.'

'Are you sure she was Brittany, and not Bethany?'

'That was it. Bethany. How did you know, Julia?'

'A hunch. Now, Jono, this is very important. What time was she there?'

'I noticed her there when we went to supper at about seven. She was looking pretty ropey even then. By the time we moved over to the bar after eating, she was very drunk. In fact, the manager guy...'

'Kevin?'

'I don't know his name.'

'Big chap. Brown hair. Gentle manner.'

'That's it. Do you know everyone's name in the whole village? And where they are at any point in time?'

Sean snorted with laughter at the question, and answered it for her: 'Pretty much.'

'No, not *everyone*,' said Julia. 'But I like to keep my eye on things. Now what were you about to say about Kevin, the manager?'

'He said she'd been there since mid-afternoon, and his impression was that she'd been somewhere else first. Another pub. He was worried about her and he had told the barman to stop serving her by the time we left. He asked her if he could call someone to fetch her, or get her a taxi, but she refused. That's when we offered to give her a lift. We were leaving and she lives not far from Laine, so Laine convinced her to come with us. We delivered her home around ten or ten thirty. Had to help her to the door and upstairs to her room. Girl was trashed.'

Julia was sorry that Bethany was in such a bad way, although it was hardly surprising. The poor girl had, after all, lost her boyfriend. Little had she realised that she would wake up to even more loss, thought Julia sadly. But she was pleased – if that was the right word – that, by Jono's account, Bethany had been drinking all afternoon and would not have been in any state to kill Roger Grave. Of course, that would depend on the time of death, too. But Julia would get hold of Walter Farmer in the morning and see if he had any more info from the forensics team.

'More dhal, dhaling?' Sean asked, nudging the carton towards Julia.

She smiled at his punny joke, but shook her head. 'Thank you, but I've had elegant sufficiency, as my gran used to say.'

'At least she didn't say "I'm stuffed", like we used to say at school lunch. It was usually followed by the loudest burp a boy could manage,' said Jono, leaning back contentedly with his hands on his tummy. 'I love a good Indian. Thanks, Dad.'

'It was a real treat, Sean,' Julia added.

'My pleasure! Now, I think it's just about time for us to be heading home. I've got early consults in the morning.'

'And I'll be up early too,' Jono said. 'I'm meeting Laine for a run. A walk-ish run. I'll take Leo.'

The dog raised his head in response to his name. Jake stirred too. The dogs had worked out fairly early on that this was not a meal that would result in a tasty chicken bone or a bit of bacon fat, and had napped through the whole thing.

'I could make us all supper sometime, if you're keen,' Jono offered shyly, looking at Julia.

'I'd really like that, Jono. Do you enjoy cooking?'

'I'm a bit out of practice the last couple of years, and haven't had much in the way of a kitchen. But I used to do a brilliant lasagne. Mum's recipe. She taught me how to make it when she was... when she got sick. Remember, Dad?'

'I do. You were about fifteen, and she said you couldn't go out into the world without a couple of wholesome recipes under your belt. That and the minestrone soup. A few others. You made the lasagne a few times for her, until you had it down, remember?'

A soft sadness passed over Jono's face. 'She couldn't eat much by then, but she gave me the thumbs-up.' He held his own thumbs up and gave a weak smile.

'What a loving thing to leave you with, Jono. Your mum gave you a real gift for life.'

Jono's eyes glistened, as if he was holding back tears.

'She did. I hadn't really thought of it like that. And I haven't had much of an opportunity to use the gift; things have been a bit...' He seemed to struggle for the right word, and he came up with the rather nebulous: 'Hard.'

Julia smiled and put her hand over his. 'It has been difficult. You're doing well, Jono. And you've got a lot of time ahead to make her lovely recipes.'

He nodded, and said briskly: 'Well, I want to get back into cooking, so I'll give that lasagne a try sometime.'

26

At exactly nine o'clock in the morning – the time her mother had drummed into her was the earliest time one might politely phone another person, outside of an emergency – Julia phoned DC Walter Farmer to tell him what she'd heard about Bethany's whereabouts on the night of Roger's death. She had thought, for a while, about whether she would be better off phoning Walter or Hayley Gibson, his superior officer. After due consideration, she'd decided that the information she had was Walter-level. Besides, Hayley was stressed and grumpy, and likely in no mood for unsolicited phone calls. Thirdly, Julia had to admit, she was motivated by the knowledge that Walter was less cagey than Hayley. She would be more likely to hear something about the investigation from him than from her.

Walter seemed pleased to hear from Julia and grateful for her information about Bethany.

'At the Swan, you say? What time?'

'She was there from sometime in the afternoon – you can check with Kevin for more exact timing – until Jono and his friend drove her home at about ten or ten thirty.'

'And she was, um, incapacitated?'

'Could barely walk, apparently. They helped her into her bedroom and onto the bed. From what they say, there's no way she went out again.'

'Right, well, I'll chat to Jono, but that seems fairly conclusive. Thanks, Julia. You've saved us some footwork.'

'Walter?'

'Yes?'

'Do you know what time Roger Grave died?'

There was a pause on the other end of the line, while Walter weighed up how much and what information to divulge. Julia could almost hear his brain clunking around in his skull on the other end of the phone. On the one hand, this was confidential police information, which he shouldn't, by rights, share with a civilian. On the other hand, Julia had been forthcoming with her own information, which created a bit of an obligation.

After some moments, Walter found a way through the conundrum. He answered: 'Let's just say that if your information is correct, Bethany could not have killed her father.'

'Well, I have done my bit for justice this morning,' Julia told Jake and Chaplin, who were regarding her with fascination and admiration. Granted, what they were fascinated by and admiring of was her ability to work the can opener or the biscuit tin and produce food at any time of the day or night. Truly, opposable thumbs were a miraculous invention. 'It seems Bethany is no longer a suspect. Poor girl.'

The pets' admiration was tinged with impatience.

'All right, here you go,' she said, clattering nuggets into Chaplin's bowl on the counter.

She opened the kitchen door to the garden. 'Now your turn, Jake.'

He needed no invitation. He shot out of the house like a bullet from a gun. Bad analogy under the circumstances, she scolded herself. He ran out of there like a chubby four-legged Usain Bolt. Julia had to tip the tin to scrape out a scoop of the last remaining dog biscuits. She poured them into his bowl, while he jumped around her feet excitedly.

Watching the pets crunch their way through their respective breakfasts, she made a mental note to buy more dog food before the weekend. Knowing that a mental note had about a fifty-fifty chance of remaining in her brain long enough to be actioned, she made another mental note to write down the contents of the first mental note when she went inside. She'd probably forget that one, too. Unless she made another mental note... And another...

She went inside and wrote 'dog food' on the list on the little pad she kept attached to the fridge with a magnet. Her mind went straight to the investigation into Roger Grave's death. Bethany had made some kind of mad sense as a suspect – if she thought her father had killed Graham, she might have been sufficiently enraged to have hit him with that book, or even thrown it at him, causing him to fall and hit his head. But if Bethany hadn't killed Roger, who had? With Bethany crossed off the list, the field of suspects might have been narrowed down, but who else was left? And more to the point – *why* had someone killed him? The matter was no closer to resolution, from what Julia could see. Roger Grave's death was a mystery.

Musing on the investigation into Roger's death, Julia realised she'd not heard anything more about the investigation into Graham's death. As Hayley had said at the time, someone was responsible for that bullet being in that gun. Either deliberately, or by oversight, someone was responsible for Graham's death. Had it been Roger? Despite what Walter had suggested about Roger's death being connected to a case he was working on, Julia was sure of one thing – when another body turns up days after a murder, you could put money on the two deaths being connected. What did Graham and Roger have in common, other than Bethany? Well, the play, of course. Julia got the funny prickly feeling she so often experienced when her brain was busy working something out, to get to a realisation, or dredge up a piece of information, or when she intuited that something was wrong.

The play. They'd both been involved in *A Night to Remember*. Graham as an actor, and Roger as director. Could there be something about the play that had led to their deaths? The prickly feeling intensified, and with it came a feeling of dread. It had been agreed by the group that the play would no longer happen, and Tabitha had let the festival organisers know. But could the other actors still be in danger?

Julia still had the pad and the stubby little pencil in her hand. She tore off the sheet with the words 'dog food' on it, and started to write names on the sheet below.

- Dylan
- Gina
- Graham
- Nicky
- Oscar
- Guy

It wasn't a long list. What about the other people involved? The ones who weren't actors? She left a space and wrote:

- Hector
- Roger

She thought for a minute, and added, feeling queasy at the thought:

- Tabitha

And then:

- Julia

Julia looked at her own name and felt that surely she was overreacting. She was completely on the wrong track. Chaplin jumped onto her lap, causing her to levitate an inch or two off the kitchen chair. 'I've let my imagination run away with me. No one from the cast is in danger,' she said to the cat, stroking his silky back while he settled himself down. He closed his eyes, letting it be known that he was only there for warmth, not conversation. She had none of his relaxed attitude to the matters of the day. The prickle was still there.

Julia's mind was churning – thinking about all she had learnt, and trying to tie it up into a logical theory about what could have happened. But she just couldn't make sense of it – and was quite relieved when the beeps of incoming messages on her phone disturbed her thoughts.

The first beep must have been the formation of a new group, and the second was Walter Farmer putting a message on the group that he had just created for the Cotswolds Players, instructing them all to report to the police station the next morning. Walter had rather cleverly made the group broadcast only, so nobody could comment on his request.

But that didn't stop the speculation starting on the main Cotswolds Players group.

What do you think he wants? asked Nicky.

Maybe we're going to the festival after all, suggested Hector.

Don't be utterly ridiculous, said Gina, who didn't usually get involved in these exchanges. *Two men have died, is that not enough for you?*

The messages volleyed back and forth, and Julia sighed.

There was nothing that any of them could do but wait and see what the police had to say. Maybe they just wanted to ask a few more questions, with everyone there. But what more could the Cotswolds Players add to what they had already told the police?

As it turned out, there was a *lot* still to say.

27

The South Cotswolds Players arranged the chairs of the police meeting room in a semicircle as they would for a cast meeting or for a read-through of the script. The half-circle faced a single chair, traditionally occupied by the director, but today by DI Hayley Gibson. She was attired, as always, in her practical uniform – dark trousers, button-up shirt, jacket, flat supportive shoes. Her short hair was a bit spiky, as if she'd been running her hands over it, and as if it might be a day past hair-wash day. Hayley wasn't one for much make-up, but she seemed to have forgotten even the little slick of mascara and touch of lip balm that she usually wore. She looked pale and harassed.

Julia sneaked a look at her watch. She hoped the meeting would be quick. She would be working at Second Chances that morning to compensate for Wednesday's absence. Having left Diane and Wilma in the lurch on Wednesday, she'd phoned to apologise profusely (Wilma was a person for whom only 'profusely' would do, when an apology was called for). She had sounded a bit scratchy, saying with a sigh, 'Oh, don't you worry, it was a busy day but Diane and I just had to manage.' And now Julia was going to be late again.

Hayley gave a brief recap of what everyone already knew without additional new information. She didn't mention Bethany. It was clear she was here to garner information, not share it.

'Given the unlikely coincidence of the two men, both involved with the Players, both dying under unusual circumstances, we are treating the deaths as suspicious. And we are examining all and any links between the two. I'm starting from scratch. Fresh eyes. Fresh ideas.'

The Players looked at Hayley expectantly.

'I want us to go back to the weeks of rehearsal leading up to Graham Powell's death,' she said. 'I want to hear the whole story again, and specifically where there was conflict. Disagreements. Fights. Misunderstandings. Even if they were minor. This is not to say anyone's going to be accused of anything. I just want to get a feel for what it was like in those rehearsals. So be honest. Let's go right back to the beginning and start with casting. How did that work?'

Nicky, unsurprisingly, was the first to put up her hand. 'So, there was a casting call. You had to email Roger if you wanted to come to casting, and fill in a form with your name, experience, age and all that.'

'Thanks, Nicky.'

'Well, if we are speaking about misunderstandings, I have to say I took a year off my age when I filled in the form. I said I was thirty-four. I've just turned thirty-five and it just sounded so... so *old*, you know? Like, middle-aged.'

She looked around for corroboration of this fact. Only Dylan, who was twenty-something, nodded in an understanding sort of way. Julia caught Tabitha's eye, but maintained a stony expression.

'I know I shouldn't have lied – well, not lied. More like a fib. I mean, it was mostly true, just a sort of adjustment of a few weeks one way or another. I didn't want to be cast as an old person. I feel bad now, honestly I do. I should have told you earlier. Come clean. I hope this hasn't muddied the waters.'

Hayley looked like a woman reconsidering her life choices. 'Thank you, Nicky. I appreciate your honesty, but I don't think it has any bearing on the case.'

It was, thought Julia, hard to imagine how Nicky believed her fib about her age could possibly have had any bearing on, well, anything really.

But Nicky looked relieved, and added, 'Also, one day, I wasn't very nice to Graham. I teased him about his trousers, the ones he wore in the play. Said he looked like a bible salesman from Tennessee. I don't know why I said that. I haven't even been to Tennessee and I don't know if they have bible salesmen there or what they look like if they do. I feel bad about that too. I hope he wasn't hurt.'

'Thank you, Nicky. Again, I don't think it relates directly to the case. Now, back to the casting. What happened after the emails?'

'There was an audition on a Saturday morning,' said Oscar. 'We all had to read a few lines. There weren't a huge number of applicants. Just about everyone who came along got a part, big or small.'

Hayley seemed relieved to have moved on to more meaty topics. 'Right. Any trouble there? In the casting, I mean.'

'Not that I saw,' said Oscar, looking round the group. 'I guess some people might have been disappointed not to get something. Or not to get a bigger or better role. But it's am-dram, after all. Not the West End. It's supposed to be a bit of fun.'

There was a glum silence after Oscar's words. Whatever fun there was supposed to have been, that had long gone.

'No conflict, then?'

'Um, do you have anything to say, Guy?' Gina said pointedly. 'A fight, perhaps?'

'I had a run-in with Roger.' The words came spilling out. All heads turned towards Guy. He was so quiet and unobtrusive that Julia tended to forget he was there at all. Let alone having run-ins with people. 'I wanted to give the Postman more personality. Even though he was a minor character, I thought he could have more gravitas. More mystery. I wanted to play him as French.'

Hector gave a dismissive snort.

'French?' Hayley's astonishment moulded the word into three distinct, lilting syllables: *Fre-e-ench?* 'Why French?'

A fair question. After all, the play was set in a manor house in 1950s England. A French postman would be unusual, to say the least.

'I do a good French accent,' said Guy, modestly, as if that explained it. He went on: ''Ello, my nem is Gee. *Je suis votre* postman...'

'*Votre facteur*,' said Dylan helpfully.

'*Facteur*? Are you sure?'

'Yes, I'm learning French on Duolingo. Funnily enough the word came up last week.'

'Well I never,' said Guy. '*Je suis votre facteur...*'

'Thank you.' Hayley held up her hand, putting an end to the excruciating performance. 'I'm assuming Roger refused?'

'He did. He didn't like the idea at all. Didn't see the point. I was quite upset and said some horrible things. Just in the heat of the moment, you know. Said he had no imagination. That he was a petty dictator. Gina must have overheard the argument.'

She nodded. 'Sorry, I don't think you killed him or anything, but the detective did say we must mention any conflict.'

Guy nodded his understanding and forgiveness, and looked down at his hands.

'Oh, I've just remembered another thing,' Nicky cut in. 'I complained to Roger about the teabags. Does that count?'

'No,' Hayley and about half the cast answered in unison.

Things continued to deteriorate after that. Despite Hayley's efforts to keep things on track, there followed an accounting of small slights, tiny tiffs, random run-ins and misunderstandings. Those weeks felt like ancient history, although they had been only a month or so ago, and the conflicts themselves entirely trivial. Julia couldn't believe that they had anything to do with the death of the two men.

Hayley called an end to the meeting, with an air of barely concealed irritation. 'Please be in touch with DC Farmer if you remember anything that might be useful. *Useful.* Nothing about teabags and French postmen and such.' She paused and spoke in a serious, measured tone: 'Now, I don't want to cause panic, but I must reiterate, the killer is still at large.'

The look on the assembled faces indicated to Julia that there was – if not panic – at least significant unease amongst some of the cast. They forgot about their trifling arguments and confessions, and focused once again on the core of the matter – two men had died, and the police didn't know how, or why, or at whose hand. The mood was suddenly sombre.

Oscar said: 'It's the men who are being targeted, isn't it? Shouldn't we have security until the murderer is behind bars? I feel rather nervous.'

'No, I don't think that's necessary at this stage. We are not at all sure what the connection is between the deaths, or if it has anything to do with this production,' said Hayley.

'Probably nothing at all. I don't think you need to be afraid, Oscar,' said Hector, with a hint of an eye-roll.

'Not afraid, just alert,' said Hayley. 'I'm just asking you all to be alert. If any of you experience anything suspicious or are at all concerned for your safety, you must phone the police immediately. I'm going to give you my personal number to save on your phones. You can of course also phone 999 in case of emergency. I don't need to tell you, this is for emergencies only.'

The players diligently tapped the digits into their phones

and then dispersed, some of them looking around anxiously as they exited the hall.

'Well, I don't know about you, but I feel better after coming clean about everything,' said Nicky, beaming at Tabitha and Julia. She didn't seem particularly troubled by the 'killer at large' speech. In fact, she seemed in excellent spirits. Having owned up to her fifth or sixth troublesome interaction, she looked like someone who'd just come out of the confessional with a clean slate and a pure soul.

Julia, who had nothing to confess, and who thought the whole exercise had been a phenomenal waste of time, returned her beam with a wan smile, and said, 'Well, I'm glad for you, Nicky.'

'Bye then, Julia. I'll be off to do my errands. Before I know it, it'll be time to fetch Sebastian.'

'I'd better dash, too. Don't want to be late for Second Chances.'

'Oh, thanks for reminding me. I broke my favourite mixing bowl. It was my grandma's, such a pretty one. You know the ones with those old-fashioned stripes? I'm so upset. I want to come over and see if you have something similar. Maybe someone else's grandma died and they didn't want her mixing bowl.'

'We usually have mixing bowls. I'll have a look when I get in and let you know.'

'Thanks, Julia. Or I'll just pop round later, or tomorrow.' Nicky bounded off with a spring in her step.

'I'll walk with you; we're going in the same direction,' said Tabitha. When she and Julia were at a decent distance from the hall, she chuckled. 'Have to say, that was one of the weirder meetings I've been to.'

'Complete waste of time for Hayley, I should think. Everyone confessing these mild transgressions and throwing themselves at her mercy.'

'Oh dear lord, Guy's story about the French postman...' Tabitha's chuckle gathered force.

'I think you mean *le facteur*...'

'*Mais oui!*'

'Oh, and the teabags!' Julia, who had been rather irritated by the whole thing, couldn't help but be drawn into her friend's good humour.

'The parking place...'

'The biscuits...'

'I had no idea there was so much strife amongst the Players.'

'I wracked my brains to find something I could confess myself,' said Julia. 'But I wasn't there with the actors enough to get into any beefs.'

'I know. Luckily, I'd been snappy about letting Gina wear her own dress, so I had something to offer.'

'I was the only person who had no transgression to speak of. Well, me and Hector.'

'Which is surprising if you think about it, because Hector is actually very... How to put it...?' Tabitha was a very kind person, always at pains not to be overly critical and never mean.

Julia helped her out. 'He's a bit annoying. So breathtakingly self-involved.'

'Yes, that, exactly. Ah well, we're none of us perfect.'

By now they were approaching Second Chances.

'Well, this is me. Bye, Tabitha. See you soon. Maybe a meal?'

'Lovely.'

They lingered for a moment at the door. There was a troubled air between them, as if something should be said. Tabitha spoke first: 'You take care of yourself, Julia. I'm sure we're not in danger, but, like Hayley said, it pays to be alert.'

'Yes, I'll keep my wits about me. You too.'

28

Wilma and Diane were busy making their morning tea when Julia arrived. Even though she'd told Wilma she would be a little late because of meeting the police, she half expected her to be all 'school prefect' about the arrival time, but instead she welcomed Julia warmly.

'Just in time for tea!' she said, leading Julia into the little storeroom which also served as kitchen, and getting out a third mug. 'Poor you, you must be exhausted with all this drama. Take the weight off your feet for a minute and help yourself to a chocolate swirl.'

Wilma shook the biscuit tin in front of Julia, who took a chocolate biscuit as instructed. Diane took the mug and poured Julia's tea. 'Here you go. How was the meeting?'

'Oh, it was fine. They just wanted to know if anyone had any additional thoughts about the two deaths. Anything at all.'

'I hoped they might have better information. A suspect, for instance,' said Diane.

'They're working on it. Hayley Gibson is a good detective. And with one of the victims being a senior police officer, all the lab technicians and forensic people are working as fast as they can.'

'You say "one of the victims". Do they think the two deaths are connected?'

Julia sipped her tea, which was exactly how she liked it. Good and hot, almost too hot, so she had to sip it gently. 'She did say that they are treating that as a possibility. It does seem likely. I mean, two men murdered within a week in a quiet little Cotswold village... It's... unusual.'

'And both of them connected to the South Cotswolds Players,' said Diane, who was quite sharp.

'Yes, although it's hard to imagine how that would be relevant. Now, how are things in the shop?'

'It's been quite quiet. One or two shoppers. Someone dropped off clothes. We'll sort these when we've had tea,' said Wilma, gesturing to a big sack on the floor. 'Another biscuit before we go?'

Julia hesitated momentarily, but it had already been a rather long morning and she had the day's work ahead of her, so she allowed herself a second biscuit, and drained her tea. They went out into the shop.

Julia remembered the mixing bowls, and checked the kitchenware section to see what they had in stock. There was rather a nice green and white striped one she thought Nicky might like. 'If Nicky Moore comes in when I'm not here, please show her this bowl,' she called to the others. 'She needs a mixing bowl and she said she'd come by.'

Speak of the devil and he shall appear, Julia's grandmother used to say. And so it was. Julia had no sooner mentioned the woman than the doorbell tinkled and Nicky appeared, rushing in in a great hurry.

'Heaven help me, I was nearly run over,' she said, in a shaking voice. 'I was crossing the road – my right of way – and this maniac in a little white car swerved and almost hit me!'

'Oh my goodness, Nicky, what a fright you must have got.' It was true; she looked quite shaken.

'He made it look like he was trying to avoid a pigeon, but I think he was trying to hit me. I think it was a deliberate attempt on my life.'

'On your *life*?' Diane said, astonished. 'My goodness.'

'Don't you know there are two people dead already? Two people connected to the play? Aren't you scared, Julia? It's like one of those Agatha Christie books, where they are locked in a train or something and people are being bumped off left, right and centre. There's a murderer on the loose! A cold-hearted man who would run a woman down in cold blood! Who cares nothing for the fact that I'm the innocent mother of a young child!'

Poor Nicky seemed to have lost her previous cool and was so shaken that Julia worried her legs might buckle underneath her and she would crash to the ground. Wilma looked somewhere between intrigued and appalled at the drama going on right in the middle of the shop. Julia decided to address both problems at once. 'Come into the back room and have a sit-down, Nicky. The kettle's still hot; I'll make you some tea, and when you're feeling stronger you can look at the mixing bowl I found for you. I think it might be just what you need.'

'Yes, I think that would be for the best. I'm in an awful state. Awful.'

Wilma smiled gratefully at Julia and added generously, 'Please, do have a chocolate swirl.'

Julia led Nicky into the back and closed the door so that any customers who might come in wouldn't overhear Nicky's retelling of her dramatic near-death experience. It did indeed sound scary. The car had been close enough to clip the bag slung over Nicky's shoulder.

They sat quietly for a minute. Julia heard the bell tinkle a couple of times, but was sure that Wilma and Diana could handle matters without her. She had her hands full with Nicky.

The tea and no fewer than three chocolate swirls seemed to settle Nicky. 'The sugar has helped, thank you, Julia,' she said. 'Shall we go and look at the mixing bowl?'

'We should phone Hayley first. She'll be able to check the street cameras and run the number plates.'

'You're right!' said Nicky, brushing crumbs from her mouth. 'I might have important information for the police.' She rummaged in her bag for her phone and dialled the number the cast had all saved.

Julia listened while Nicky repeated the story she'd told Julia, a bit more calmly this time. After a few minutes, she ended the call and said, 'DI Gibson was grateful for my information. She's following up on those cameras as a priority, she says. A *priority*. I hope to see that maniac behind bars! Terrible man.'

The sight of the mixing bowl went some way to further calming Nicky and improving her day.

'It's perfect!' she said, hugging it to her chest as if it were a long-lost child. 'It's almost identical to my grandma's bowl. The same green stripe. Oh, thank you, Julia.' Her eyes glistened with tears.

'You are most welcome, Nicky. It was really just good luck!'

'Well, I do feel lucky to have such a thoughtful friend.' She put the bowl down on the counter, hugged Julia, and pulled out her purse. 'How much is it?'

Julia was overcome with a feeling of generosity and love for poor Nicky, who had had a scary day. 'Nothing. I'm going to buy it for you. It's my treat.'

'Oh, now Julia, you can't do that...'

'I can and I will. It's always best to have a little nice thing after a horrible thing. To cancel it out.'

Nicky hugged Julia again, carefully put the bowl in her carrier bag, and went off with a spring in her step.

'I'll pop the money in the till when we cash up,' Julia said to Wilma.

'That's kind of you, Julia. I'll give you the staff discount, of course. And a bit extra.'

For the rest of the afternoon, Julia felt the warm flush that comes with doing a small good deed that makes someone else happy. Wilma and Diane seemed likewise infused with good-will, and the rest of the day passed happily. They sorted the newest donations. Dusted the window display. Sold a nice set of crystal glasses to Mrs Glenn who lived in the manor, and a stupendously ugly china corgi dog to a woman who lived in Wisconsin. Found a pretty silk shift dress for a cash-strapped young woman to wear to a better-off friend's wedding, and gave her a discount just to be nice. The day passed pleasantly, and in the quiet of the mid-afternoon, Wilma suggested that if Julia had things to do, it would be fine for her to leave.

'I think I will, if you're sure you can manage,' Julia said, glancing over at the shop's one customer – an old fellow reading a gardening book, seemingly from cover to cover. He'd been there an hour. 'Oh, let me pay you for the bowl, before I go.'

'Six pounds,' said Wilma. 'Five with the discount.'

Julia handed over the cash.

'I must say, it's been a good day,' Wilma said. 'The highest turnover we've done in a while, even with the discounts.'

'Really?'

'Yes, more sales than usual, and some expensive items. Those glasses were quite a price, and the china dog, too. We even sold an expensive book. Five pounds.'

'What second-hand book was worth such a princely sum?' Julia asked, as she packed up her bag. The shop was the recip-ient of a great number of books, many boxes of them from clear-outs and downsizing, and death. Supply outstripped demand and the majority sold for a pound at most.

'Nothing less than the bard himself!' said Diane, with a laugh. 'It was a lovely big old edition of *The Complete Works of Shakespeare*. Someone's got their work cut out for them if they're planning to read the whole thing. It's a whopper, I tell you, and the print is tiny.'

Wilma snorted dismissively. 'I suspect no one reads those books. Apart from anything else, it weighs a tonne. Can you imagine holding that up when you're reading in bed?'

'Or in the bath,' Diane chimed in. 'Imagine that.'

'I reckon the chap that bought it is going to use it as decoration, or perhaps as a doorstop.'

Julia's brain whirred around the strange coincidence of this book coming into her life twice in a week. It couldn't be chance.

'So, who bought it?' she asked, hoping she sounded casual. Perhaps it was some tourist, she thought suddenly. They did tend to buy strange and pricey souvenirs. They might have got Berrywick confused with Stratford-upon-Avon.

But the answer, when Wilma gave it, was not a misdirected tourist.

The answer was far, far closer to the murder than that.

Hector.

29

Julia was thoroughly discombobulated by what she'd heard at Second Chances. She had hardly had time to think through what it might mean that it was Hector who had purchased *The Complete Works of Shakespeare* from the second-hand shop. This was not a case of someone unconnected to the deaths randomly buying a copy of the very book that was the murder weapon. This was someone who was very, very close to the case.

She had to put aside one set of uncomfortable feelings and thoughts for another as she stopped off at the vet, knowing that the long-time receptionist, Olga Gilbert, was no longer going to be at the counter. She was no longer anywhere, the poor thing. She was dead. Both her and one of the vets, Dr Eve. Julia may have had a hand in solving their murders, but she still felt peculiar every time she walked into the vet's reception. It felt particularly strange now, as her brain grappled with another murder.

'Oh, hello.' It was the new receptionist. She sounded surprised, as if she hadn't been expecting visitors. She looked about fifteen years old, an impression not in any way countered by the rhythmic movement of her jaw engaged with a piece of gum, and the presence of an iPhone in front of her face. She lowered the phone, popped a little bubble between her back teeth, and asked Julia: 'Can I help you?'

Julia asked for a bag of Jake's preferred dog food, Pheasant Flavour Doggy Chum.

'Oh, gosh, I don't see any here,' the receptionist said, putting the phone down on the desk reluctantly and glancing over at the shelves of pet food. 'I think they might have the Pheasant Flavour, but it's in the storeroom.' She gave Julia an apologetic look, as if she was sorry they'd come to this dead end, but there was nothing to be done.

'Well, could we get it out of the storeroom, perhaps?' Julia asked. 'Or isn't there a key?'

'Oh, yes. There's a key.' The girl looked at Julia blankly and went back to chewing her gum.

'Do you have it? The key?'

'I think it's in the drawer.' She opened the drawer unhurriedly and picked up a key with a red tag, marked STORE-ROOM. 'Here it is.'

'Let's get the dog food out then, shall we?'

Julia used the plural, but expected the receptionist to bestir herself and fetch the food. Instead, the girl handed over the key and said, 'Go through to the back room. The food is in the big cupboard on the right; just open it and see what you can find.'

Julia felt fairly sure this wasn't the customer's job, but her interactions with the girl had been so unsatisfactory so far that she thought she might as well just fetch the food herself. She wandered through to the back room, where she came across Dr Ryan at a little table doing some paperwork.

He looked startled to see her. 'Hello, Mrs Bird. Everything all right? Are you here with Jake? Why are you...?'

She held up the key. 'Jake's fine; I'm just here for his food. I was sent back here to get Pheasant Flavour Doggy Chum – there's none at the front.'

'I'm sorry,' he said, jumping to his feet. 'Let me get it for you. This temp is hopeless, I'm afraid. Even so, I can't believe she is sending the customers to do errands.'

Julia handed him the key with its red tag. 'I don't really mind, but I must say it was a bit of a surprise.'

'Well, she's been here for a week and today is her last day. Apart from anything else, it turns out she doesn't like dogs! She's scared of them. Can you imagine anyone not liking dogs? Let alone not liking dogs and taking a temp job at a vet's? I'll have to ask the agency to send someone else. Someone a bit more sensible. Someone who likes dogs.'

Dr Ryan sighed. He went into the storeroom and came out with a bag of dog food hefted under his arm. He looked so unhappy.

'I'm sure you miss Olga. She was so efficient. And she loved dogs.'

'I do miss Olga. And Dr Eve. It's been difficult, actually, getting on with work without them.'

They shared a moment's silence at the memory of the two women, and then went into the reception area. A woman and a little boy were waiting. The boy had a large rat in a cage on his knee. The rat had a bandage on its leg.

'Hello, Tom; hello, Ratty. I'll be with you in a mo,' said Dr Ryan. To the receptionist, he said, 'Please ring this up; I'll take it to Mrs Bird's car.'

Julia went out to the car with him and opened the boot. Poor Dr Ryan, having to make do with such terrible staff on top of a doubled workload. And now he was carrying dog food to the car. It was a pity he couldn't find someone permanent to replace Olga. Someone reliable. Someone who loved animals, and dogs in particular. He needed someone young and cheery; but not *too* young or *too* cheery.

Julia was struck by a good idea. Well, she thought it was a good idea. She hesitated, though. It wasn't without risk. Oh, what the heck, might as well give it a go, she thought. The events of the past week or so had made her feel bolder, more eager to grasp the moment, because honestly, who knew what the future held? She addressed the vet: 'I know someone who I think would be perfect for your reception. He's a young man who has just moved back to the area and is looking for temporary work to start with. He is quite sensible and absolutely brilliant with dogs. Jake adores him.'

'Please ask him to phone me. He can't possibly be as dim as this poor girl.'

'I can tell you for certain that you wouldn't have to worry that he'd send a customer to get a big bag of dog food from the storeroom herself.'

'He sounds like a genius. I look forward to his phone call.'

On the drive home from the vet, Julia thought about Hector, and his recent purchase. She knew he liked his Shakespeare. In fact, hadn't he boasted that he'd learnt all the lines of all the plays? Something like that. But presumably he already had a copy of the *Collected Works*. Or at least the individual plays. How would he have learnt them otherwise? And why would he be buying another? Unless...

Unless he'd lost his copy. Julia could still see the scene of Roger Grave's death, the book lying next to his body, its flattened corner matching a bruise from the blow to his temple. Could Hector have hit Roger Grave over the head with the heavy book? If so, his original copy was in the forensics lab, and he was now in possession of a replacement, purchased at Second Chances.

She reached instinctively for her phone. This was something she needed to tell Hayley Gibson about. While her hand was digging in the well between the seats, her mind was racing to the next logical thought about Hector. A bicycle turned into the road. The cyclist took the turn a little wide and wobbled too close to her. Distracted by her thoughts and the search for her phone, Julia saw him only just in time to avoid him. The near miss shocked her into concentration. She abandoned her scrabble for the phone and put both hands on the wheel, both eyes on the road, and her mind on the job of getting home safely. When she got there, she would phone Hayley Gibson and tell her about Hector and the book.

The more she thought about it, the more suspicious she felt, and the more sure she was that Hector had been the one wielding the heavy book. But why? Hector had been disappointed about the casting of the play, but that surely was no reason to kill a person? And where did Graham's death fit in? Even if Hector had thrown the Shakespeare at Roger in a fit of rage, why on earth would he have killed Graham?

As soon as she parked the car, she found her phone and searched for Hayley's number. She hit the 'dial' button as she got out of the car. Hayley answered before she'd reached the front door.

'Hello, Julia.'

'Hello.'

'I suppose you are phoning about Nicky's hit-and-run.' Hayley wasn't much one for a preamble. Straight to the point, was the DI. 'Well, you can relax. We watched the tapes. The alleged would-be male murderer was a little old lady swerving to avoid a pigeon. She missed Nicky by miles. It was not an attempt on her life, as she thought.'

'Ah, well, that's good news, I suppose, but that's not why I was phoning... It's...'

Julia stopped, sensing movement from the path behind her. There were two figures coming towards her. It was already heading for dusk, and she couldn't see the faces, but by their shape, it seemed they were men. It was a sad reality that even in sleepy Berrywick, the sight of two unknown men on a quiet road could make a woman feel uneasy.

But Julia had a horrible feeling she knew who it was. And if she was right, she might well be in far more danger than she had initially thought.

Hector and Troilus came into view.

But Hector didn't look at all aggressive. In fact, he approached with a friendly smile on his face. Troilus trailed behind, his face blank, and Julia briefly wondered if Hector worried about him the way that Sean worried about Jono.

'Hello, Hector,' she spoke loudly, to make sure that Hayley could hear, and would know who was there with her. 'Hello, Troilus. Give me a minute, please.'

Speaking into the phone, she said, 'I can't chat, there's someone here, a surprise visitor. I just wanted to let you know I'm at home, so you are welcome to pop round as we discussed. Okay, bye.'

He was right by her now, a big canvas satchel hanging heavily from his shoulder. She wondered if the book was in it, and what else might be. Did he have a weapon, perhaps?

'Can I help you, Hector?' she said, with what she hoped was a calm smile.

'Yes, hello. We were out for a walk and I remembered that you lived around here, and I told Troilus about you, Julia. How you provided so much of the set and props from the charity shop where you work, and how you've even helped the police solve several murders, and how you have such a wonderful dog. And then Troilus suggested we continue past your house so that I could show him the dog. I hope I didn't startle you.'

Troilus looked absolutely blank at this story, which Julia thought he well might – it was such an odd and unlikely story that she suspected Hector had made it up on the spot. But why? Why mention the charity shop? The charity shop where just today he had bought a replacement copy of Shakespeare. Was he trying to threaten her by mentioning it? That, and the solving of murders? It all seemed far too spot-on to be a coincidence.

'Not at all,' she said, trying for a breezy tone that would reassure Hector that she suspected nothing. Although she did suspect something – she suspected that Hector had come here on purpose.

Julia was scared.

She told herself not to panic, that she was probably overreacting. After all, Hector hadn't seen her at the shop today; he didn't know that she knew he had bought a replacement Shakespeare. Still, there was something odd about this visit. She hoped against hope that Hayley Gibson had heard her, and got the message – that Julia was at home, and Hector was there, and she needed her help.

Hector continued as if he was just out for a chat. 'It was a hard day, wasn't it? The cast meeting upset me, rather. The fragility of life, the unpredictability. It's so *confronting*,' he mused.

'Yes, it was hard. To think that two of our number are dead.'

'"The time of life is short!" to quote *Henry IV*. The Bard, of course...'

'Yes, indeed, and made significantly shorter, in the case of Graham and Roger.'

'Awful. Just awful, what happened, Julia. But life must go on.'

'Indeed it must!'

Standing there on the doormat, they could hear Jake's whining and the scratch of his feet as he turned excited circles on the other side of the door. Julia found the front door key on the bunch in her hand and held it to the lock, ready to let herself in.

'The dog!' said Hector. 'How silly of me. You wanted to see him, didn't you, Troy?'

Troilus seemed to rouse himself. 'Definitely,' he said. 'I would like to go in and see that dog.'

Julia didn't want Hector or Troilus in her house. She

suspected – strongly suspected – that Hector had been responsible for Roger's death. But if she said no, he might realise she
suspected him, and that would definitely put her in danger. She
tried a different tack.

'I'm really sorry, but Jake is so impossible with visitors. He
gets completely overexcited; a visitor can set him off for the
whole night.'

'I really, really want to see that dog,' said Troilus. He looked
at Julia like a child who had been denied a treat.

Julia sighed. Perhaps the lad really did have a sudden need
to meet Jake, and the timing was just unfortunate. Surely
Hector wouldn't threaten her in front of his son?

Realising that she had no option – other than saying
outright 'I think your father might be a murderer and I won't let
him into my house' – she unlocked the door and went in. She
left it open behind them, to reinforce the fact that this was a
short pop-in to meet Jake, and – her heart raced when she had
this thought – in case she needed to run.

Jake didn't let her down on the overexcitement front. He
hurled himself about the place like a loon. A loon who'd been
locked in a dark cellar for a week, and was starved of human
company.

'Ah, what a good boy,' said Hector, rubbing Jake's head
enthusiastically. 'Look at him, Troy. Isn't he a fine boy!'

'He's very nice,' said Troilus, who barely seemed to be
looking at the dog. 'Very brown.'

'Well, you made us come all this way, Troilus,' said Hector.
'Give the dog a pat.'

Julia recognised the exasperation that only a parent could
feel with a frustrating child. Usually though, the child in question was a bit younger than Troilus. It was almost like he had
frozen at the age he was when his mother died. Hector put his
satchel down on the table with a thump.

Chaplin, who was sitting on the table, hissed in Hector's

direction as the bag went down. It was true that Chaplin tended to be entitled and supercilious, but Julia had never seen or heard him hiss at anyone. Was this some kind of sign? Was Chaplin some kind of savant cat who could detect evil the same way as those people who could find water with twigs?

Now she really was being ridiculous, she told herself sternly. The cat was simply annoyed at the disturbance.

She tried to reassure herself again that Hector couldn't know that she knew he had bought the *Complete Works*. She was pretty sure he hadn't seen her at Second Chances when he was there earlier. As far as he was aware, she knew nothing about the book, and wasn't busy constructing theories about his involvement in Roger's murder.

His next statement seemed to be innocuous enough: 'Sorry, cat. I didn't mean to bother you.'

Chaplin gave him a withering look and turned away. Hector seemed unperturbed by the cat's behaviour. Troilus had finally roused himself into action, and bent down to give Jake a pat. 'Good dog,' he said. Jake's tail thumped with pleasure. A pat was a pat, no matter how unexpected the person delivering it.

Hector, to Julia's dismay, pulled out a chair and sat down, smiling benignly at Troilus.

'Such a tragedy, Roger's death,' he said. 'And Graham's. And things always come in threes.'

Julia froze. The man was absolutely cold-blooded! He sat there with a smile on his face, as good as telling her that she would be the third death. Julia reached out and held on to the back of one of the chairs to steady herself.

'Hector, I really think...'

But Hector, as ever, had no interest in what anyone else thought.

Hector had only one thing on his mind.

30

'Yes, indeed, things always happen in threes,' Hector said, with a deep sigh. 'One,' he held up his finger to illustrate. 'Graham. Two: Roger. And three: Shakespeare.'

Julia, who had been wondering if she would be able to grab a kitchen knife to defend herself, found herself staring at the man, open-mouthed.

'Shakespeare?' Surely Shakespeare's death had been too long ago to warrant being included in this list?

'Would you believe that this week, of all weeks, my *Complete Works* went missing? Just as I needed the soothing voice of the Bard to still the sorrow in my heart, it was nowhere to be found. Completely misplaced.'

'Hector...'

'But all was not lost. I found a marvellous copy in your lovely little charity shop. Dare I say it, an even more beautiful version than my own. Ah, how I look forward to rereading the great works and annotating them as I did before. The Lord giveth, the Lord taketh away. Or in this case, tooketh and then gaveth.' Hector gave a slight frown, trying to correctly express the machinations of the deity.

Julia sat herself down in the chair she had been holding on to. If Hector was telling her about his lost Shakespeare, she must have been wrong. There was no chance that he would be sharing this unless he genuinely believed that his book was lost, and not a murder weapon. The police had deliberately not shared this piece of the puzzle – nobody except Julia, the police and the murderer knew about the book.

And if it wasn't Hector, then someone had taken the book from him, and used it to throw at Roger. It was hard to imagine that someone had taken it specifically to use as a murder weapon – but perhaps the plan had been to leave it on the scene to frame Hector – which is exactly what it had done.

'Hector,' she said, in her firmest and most commanding voice. 'There's something you should know.'

Hector's eyes grew rounder and rounder as Julia explained that a copy of the *Complete Works* had been found next to Roger's body. He clasped his chest theatrically.

'Felled by the Bard?' he said, in clear distress. 'By my very own book. Oh, Julia, how can this possibly be?'

'Well, I think the real question is, who could have taken your book?'

'Nobody,' said Hector, confidently.

'And yet, someone did. You just told me that it was missing.'

'It was in my house, next to my bed. Nobody could get in. The book was just mislaid somehow. Troilus is home most of the time; he would have seen. Wouldn't you, Troilus?'

Troilus.

Julia had all but forgotten Troilus, in her conversation with Hector. But now she turned to look at him.

He stood frozen, staring at them. She might have thought he hadn't heard anything that they had said, except for a lone tear that made its way down his cheek.

'Oh, Papa,' he said. 'You always trust people far too much.' He shook his head slowly. 'Why did you even tell Julia about your missing book? She seems like such a nice lady, and now I'm going to have to sort her out.'

'Sort her out?' said Hector. 'What on earth are you talking about, Troilus?'

But Julia had put together the puzzle much more quickly, and knew exactly what Troilus meant. Her heart was hammering in her ears, knowing what danger she was in. She understood how to deal with troubled young men professionally, and now her life depended on that skill.

'You were just trying to help your father, weren't you, Troilus?' she said, standing up, hoping her voice betrayed none of her fear. She couldn't have been completely successful, because Jake sat up from where he had been lying next to Troilus, and came over to her. She put a hand on his head, drawing strength from her loyal friend.

'It's true. I never meant any of this to happen. Papa just needed help.'

Troilus looked so sad and at sea. Julia knew he had probably had years of feeling lonely and being misunderstood. From his perspective, it was simply another situation where nobody understood what he was trying to do.

'The best thing to do is to speak to the police. Tell them everything. Explain what happened.'

'I didn't mean to kill Mr Grave, you know.' Troilus said this almost conversationally.

'What?' gasped Hector, who seemed to be several steps behind the conversation.

'I never thought you did,' Julia said gently.

'You didn't?'

'Of course not.'

Troilus gave her a tiny smile, grateful for that small show of faith. 'I only went to his house to talk to him. To find out why he never cast Papa in anything. I brought the book so I could show him how hard Papa works, how much he loves the stage. All the notes he made. My papa is a very great actor, and I just wanted Mr Grave to understand that.'

'Oh, my darling boy,' said Hector softly, finally understanding. 'What have you done?'

'I spoke to him and tried to explain. But then he said...' Troilus paused, as if seeking the strength to repeat what he had heard. 'He said that Papa wasn't any good. Oh, he tried to pretend he wasn't saying anything bad, said how valuable Papa was as the prompt. But he said Papa is a terrible actor.' Troilus let out a sob.

'That must have been hard to hear, Troilus,' Julia said. 'I'm sorry.'

'It was. It was a lie! Papa is wonderful. He knows *all* the Shakespeare, all of it! Nobody else can say that, can they?'

'Hector is certainly remarkable,' said Julia.

'Anyway, he said...' Troilus closed his eyes for a moment, and it was clear that he was remembering words almost too horrible to repeat. 'He said Papa was the worst actor he has ever seen.'

Julia nodded and made soothing affirmative noises.

'Papa was on television, you know. He was a great star. Did you know that, that my papa was on the telly?'

'Yes, of course. It has been mentioned.' Mostly by Hector himself, but Julia didn't say that. Nor did she mention that his character had been in a coma for most of the show's run and he had done next to no acting. Troilus looked pleased to hear that Hector's fame was well-known.

Hector had stood up and was looking at Troilus, tears streaming down his face. 'Oh, Troilus, you didn't...'

Julia thought her heart might break for Hector. The terrible and unique pain of realising that your child has done something bad and irreversible, and that they have done it for you. She could hardly imagine what he must be feeling.

'I knew if he could hear Papa do Hamlet he'd change his

mind. I showed him all Papa's notes in the book. But he cut me off, really quite abruptly. Rudely. I just got so mad. I saw red. I threw the book at him.'

Troilus stopped talking, breathing heavily in rough, rasping gulps. Julia waited, holding her tongue. His breath evened out and his shoulders softened. He spoke quietly. 'I threw the book at him. He wanted me to leave, he was walking to the door, so he was in front of me. And I threw it. I can't throw well. I don't do *sports*. I couldn't hit him if I tried. And I didn't try, just threw it. I couldn't believe it when it hit him on the head just as he turned to look back at me. I can still see his face. The surprise, and then he just looked blank. His knees buckled and he went down slowly. And then the *crack*. His head hit the table. And that was that. He was dead.' Troilus turned to Hector. 'I'm sorry, Papa. I know you liked him.'

'You didn't mean to kill him.' Julia spoke softly and calmly.

'No. You don't expect to kill someone with a *book*!'

'Of course you don't. It's the most ineffectual murder weapon imaginable. You must tell DI Gibson exactly what you've told me. She will understand, Troilus. And I've no doubt the lab results will bear out your version of events.'

His whole demeanour lightened. 'Do you really think so?'

'Yes, Troilus, I really do. The head injury will be consistent with a fall, and the accidental blow to his head from the hall table. I don't think there's any chance you will be convicted for Roger's death.' Of course, Graham's killing – which she felt certain must also have been Troilus's work – was another matter. She hoped to avoid that topic altogether, but Hector must have had the same thought at the same time, because he looked at his son.

'Troilus, did you kill Mr Powell too? Please tell me you didn't.'

His face hardened. 'Yes. Mr Powell needed to die so you could get the role, Papa. Obviously.' Troilus said this like he couldn't quite imagine why anyone would have an issue with it. 'You didn't like Mr Powell, Papa. You said he was a very bad actor. You said if only something would happen to him, you would get your big chance. That's what you said.'

'I didn't mean I wanted him killed, for God's sake,' said Hector. 'I meant that I hoped he got a touch of flu or something. Possibly a sprained ankle.'

'How was I supposed to know that? I did it for you, Papa,' said Troilus sadly. 'You should be a bit more grateful.'

Julia realised that Troilus was actually dangerously unhinged. His sense of right and wrong was not quite the same as other people's, and Hector was the centre of his strange world.

'I *had* to get rid of him,' Troilus repeated. 'Even though in the end, it didn't work. You didn't even get the part, thanks to stupid Mr Grave. And then they cancelled the play. After I sorted out Mr Grave. It was all for nothing, Papa.'

Troilus looked around, blinking. 'Now you know what happened, Julia Bird. When Papa told me that you worked at the shop, and helped the police solve murders, I knew that you'd figure it out. That's why we had to come and see you, you know. I don't really like dogs, actually.'

This was not good. Julia knew that she was in grave danger. Troilus was not a sane man. He would never hurt Hector, but he would certainly hurt her, and feel nothing for it. She carefully backed towards the kitchen counter, where she knew her heavy kettle stood.

She didn't have to wait long for the threat to become explicit.

'I'm sorry to say, Julia Bird, that I'm going to have to get rid of you too.'

'No, Troilus, you do *not* have to do anything more,' said Hector, desperately reaching out to his son. 'We'll just explain to the police about what happened, and about how you were just doing it for me, and I'm sure that a good lawyer will get you off. No need to hurt nice Julia, is there, my darling boy?'

Troilus sighed, as if he couldn't believe his father was this naive. He pushed Hector away and reached for the satchel on the table.

Well, Julia wasn't going to wait around for him to throw the *Complete Works* at her head, or haul out whatever crazy murder weapon he planned to use on her.

Her fingers made contact with the curved handle of the kettle. She grasped it firmly and swung it towards him. She heard the slosh of water hitting inside it as she let go.

And she heard another thing. A familiar voice saying: 'There'll be no more murders, Troilus. Now, put your hands on your head and...'

For a moment, time seemed to stand still. It was as if everything and everyone were suspended: DI Hayley Gibson at the front door, her face set into a stern frown, her arm reaching in the direction of Troilus, Hector leaning towards Troilus – it was unclear whether to stop him or protect him – but his eyes still looking back towards Julia and the kettle, the kettle leaving Julia's hand, winging its way towards Troilus.

Julia saw it all frozen for a brief second, as if fixed in Perspex, and then all the pieces began to move again, continuing their trajectories.

The kettle connected with Troilus's chest just as Hector's hand grasped his shoulder to pull him back, and Hayley grasped his arm. Julia instinctively stepped forward, followed closely by Jake. Jake's feet scrabbled on the floor, wet from the kettle, and he barked a bark she'd never heard before – loud and sharp and angry.

The kettle hit Troilus hard, and for a moment he wavered between keeping his balance and falling, but the wet floor had the final say, and his feet slid out from under him. He fell so fast, and with such force, that Hayley and Hector both lost hold of him. Struggling to stay upright herself, Julia watched Hayley launch herself at Troilus, using her weight to keep him down, stopping him from making any further moves towards Julia.

But he didn't move.

The fight had gone out of him. He let out a small, sad utterance, somewhere between a shout and a wail. Jake gave him a warning growl, but it wasn't really necessary – Troilus's whole attitude was one of defeat. There would be no further danger from him.

'Oh, my boy, my boy,' said Hector, wringing his hands, looking at the scene of chaos. 'What have you done!'

Jake growled again.

'It's okay, Jakey,' Julia said, patting her leg to call him away. Chaplin watched from the counter, as if presiding over the scene from the pulpit.

When Hayley Gibson spoke, it was with her hand on Troilus's shoulder in gentle restraint that appeared almost like a priest giving her blessing: 'You do not have to say anything. But, it may harm your defence if you do not mention when questioned something which you later rely on in court. Anything you do say may be given in evidence.'

Hector sobbed quietly as he watched his son slowly stand up.

'I did it for you, Papa,' Troilus said, as Hayley led him away.

31

'What do you know about Hayley's guest?' asked Sean. The knife slicing through the cucumber that he was cutting for the salad beat a rhythmic percussion on the wooden board underneath.

'Her guest? Her significant other?' Jono said with a teasing smile. 'Her special friend?'

His father laughed, acknowledging his curiously old-fashioned terminology. 'I never know what one's supposed to call anyone these days. I mean, it's a new relationship, so I don't want to say girlfriend...'

'Don't pay any attention to your son's teasing, Sean. Guest is fine, or friend,' Julia said, rubbing his shoulder. 'To answer your question, I know very little about her. I know that her name is Sylvia, but that's about it. You know what Hayley is like: she plays her cards close to her chest. The only reason I know about the relationship at all is because I spotted evidence of an admirer when I was in her office – first an orchid, which appeared on her desk, and then a very nice fruit basket which I happened to see being delivered. I put two and two together.'

'It's almost like you're a detective yourself.' It was Sean's turn to tease now. He addressed Julia with a grin. 'Picking up clues, putting things together, solving mysteries...'

'Arresting murderers,' Jono said. He opened the oven door and inserted a huge vegetarian lasagne that he'd prepared the day before. He shut the door firmly, with an air of quiet satisfaction.

'Oh, come now, I didn't arrest any murderers. Hayley did that.' Julia shut the cutlery drawer sharply with her hip. In her hands, she held a spiky bouquet of knives and forks. 'But I did identify the likely presence of an admirer, and when we were wrapping up the Troilus business, Hayley sort of apologised for being so gruff and absent the last few weeks. She said that she had been completely caught up with the two murders and a new relationship. That's when I asked them both for lunch today. To be honest, I was a little surprised when Hayley accepted and seemed eager to bring her new girlfriend. Surprised, but pleased, and a bit intrigued.'

Julia had never known Hayley to have a partner, and had no idea what sort of person she would find appealing. So yes, she was rather looking forward to meeting Sylvia.

'Well, all will soon be revealed!' said Jono. He had been in very good humour since he and Sean had arrived to put the lasagne in the oven and help Julia with the preparations for lunch.

Laine was coming for lunch, too, and Julia suspected that her imminent arrival was at least partly responsible for Jono's good mood. Sean's mind seemed to have been following a similar trajectory, because he said, 'Is Laine bringing her goat to lunch?'

'Of course not. You can't take goats to other people's houses,' said Jono dismissively, as if it was a ridiculous idea – somehow more ridiculous than walking around Berrywick with a goat on a leash. 'You can't take them anywhere, goats. They eat everything. Plants, vegetables, bread rolls, washing off the line. Bringing a goat with you is a sure way of ruining a friend-ship, according to Laine.'

'It sounds as if she's had direct experience,' said Sean, who had finished with the cucumber and was now slicing baby toma-toes. He had a surgeon's precision with a knife, cutting each one lengthways from top to bottom in two perfectly equal halves. Julia would have done them twice as fast, but a lot less perfectly. Each to his own, she thought.

'Yes.' Jono rolled his eyes dramatically. 'It did not end well, believe me.'

Julia would have liked to hear more detail about the friend-ship-ending goat visit, but before she could enquire, the kitchen door opened and Tabitha came in, a basket hanging from the crook of her elbow. 'I came a bit early,' she said. 'I thought I could lend a hand, but it looks as if you have plenty of hands.'

'We do, but I'm glad you're here early.' Julia hugged her friend. From her basket, Tabitha produced a round country loaf, studded with seeds. 'Home-made,' she said proudly, handing it over. 'I've finally got the hang of the sourdough thing.'

'Clever you. Gosh, this looks marvellous!' said Julia. She passed Tabitha the cutlery that was still in her hands. 'You set the table, and I'll find a board for the bread.'

The salad was made and the table set when Hayley arrived, accompanied by a young woman with honey-blonde hair and a sweet, heart-shaped face. She was dressed in a long floral dress with a fitted bodice and floaty skirt, and she carried a bunch of flowers that matched the floral pattern almost exactly.

'This is Sylvia,' Hayley said. 'Sylvia, this is Julia.' Sylvia gave Julia an almost-hug and handed over the flowers. 'And this is Sean, and Jono.' Hayley pointed them out in turn. 'And that's Tabitha.'

There was a flurry of hellos. The welcome Sylvia received was so effusive that it felt rather awkward. Fortunately, Laine arrived and attention shifted to her, and then to drinks, which

Sean offered and poured. Julia appreciated the way he played co-host when they entertained at her house. It felt warm and comfortable.

Jake, who had been banished from the kitchen, joined them all in the sitting room. He calmly took his place in front of the sofa where Jono sat with Laine, and lay down between their two sets of feet with a sigh. Leo was already happily asleep in a patch of sunlight.

'Aren't they lovely chaps?' Sylvia said.

'Do you have dogs, Sylvia?' Julia asked, making conversation.

'Not at the moment. I would love to, but I'm at work most of the day, so it doesn't seem fair. Besides, I spend all day with seven-year-olds, who are basically like puppies. Energetic, full of fun, exhausting, cute as buttons.'

Jono laughed. 'You're a teacher?'

'Yes, I am. I love it, honestly I do.' She beamed. She had a lovely, lively energy, and a sweet lightness to her. She and Hayley must have been in the 'opposites attract' camp. Hayley was intense and driven, and while she could be funny and kind, no one had ever accused her of lightness.

'What do you do for work, Jono?' asked Sylvia.

Julia felt a jolt of worry for poor Jono. Sylvia had asked the question with warmth and genuine interest, but it was an awkward one, given that he was an unemployed failed musician currently living with his dad.

Surprisingly, he beamed at Sylvia and answered eagerly. 'Well, I suppose this is a good time to tell everyone that I'm starting a new job on Monday!'

'What?' Sean looked amazed at this news. Clearly, Jono hadn't told him. He was a dark horse, that young man.

'I'll be working at the reception at our local vet. I phoned Dr Ryan yesterday and we chatted and they asked me to come in on Monday. It's a temp job, really. I'll be on trial for a few weeks. But if I like it and they like me, we'll make it official.'

'That's absolutely brilliant news!' said Julia. 'Well done, Jono.'

'Well, thanks for the lead. You're the one who told me they were looking.'

'Oh, that's my pleasure. They're lucky to have you.' She turned to Sylvia and explained, 'Jono is an absolute dog whisperer. If he wasn't here, Jake would be running around whacking our drinks out of our hands with his tail. And look, he's perfectly calm.'

'What a wonderful skill to have,' Sylvia laughed. 'You should come to my class, see if you can do the same with kids. Perfectly calm sounds nice, at least every now and then.'

Jono blushed. 'I'm sure small humans are way beyond my abilities. Now, if you'll excuse me, I'll go and check on the lasagne.'

'A lasagne whisperer, too? You're a man of many talents,' said Laine. 'I'll come and help you, shall I?'

Jono practically bounced out of the room, a big grin on his face, with Laine following close behind him. If it was possible, Sean looked even happier than Jono. Julia caught his eye, and they did a small pantomime of microexpressions indicating surprise and happiness and the promise of a full discussion on the matter as soon as they were alone.

'Now, Hayley,' Tabitha said, who had clearly been waiting for the opportunity to address the important matter of the day. 'I heard that you arrested Troilus. Can you tell us any more? Whatever isn't confidential, I mean.'

'The press is all over it, as you can imagine. It will be in all the papers tomorrow, so there's no need for secrecy,' Hayley said. 'I can tell you that Troilus has been arrested for both murders. The evidence is pretty overwhelming.'

'But why?' said Sylvia. 'I don't understand.'

Julia answered slowly. 'Troilus had a really difficult child-hood. His mother died when he was young, and his world has centred around Hector, who protected him and looked after him, not always disciplining him when he should have. They had both lost the person they loved most, and it made them even closer to each other. Too close, some might argue.'

'But what made him want to kill those men?' asked Sylvia. 'Not every traumatised young man ends up murdering people.'

'You're quite right. It would probably never have happened if it wasn't for the show. Troilus saw how desperately Hector wanted a bigger part, and I think that he saw a way he could finally help his father, like his father always helped him. Troilus killed Graham thinking that with him gone, and with Hector himself knowing the lines, he'd get the lead role.'

'That's right,' said Hayley. 'It seems that he was often around at rehearsals, skulking about the hall, or backstage. Nobody really noticed him after a while.'

'That's so true,' said Julia. 'When we had to list the people involved in the show, we didn't even think of Troilus. We all treated him like Hector's shadow. Maybe if we hadn't...' Julia felt herself getting upset again, as she did every time she thought about how their dismissive attitude to Troilus had almost helped him get away with not one, but two murders.

Sean reached out a comforting hand. 'You couldn't have known, Julia.'

'You certainly couldn't have,' said Hayley firmly.

'So, what happened, exactly?' Sylvia asked Hayley. 'How did he do it?'

'He knew that Oscar pulled the trigger in the final scene. He'd seen him do it in the dress rehearsal. He was one of those children who collected odd objects that he found – fossils and broken trinkets and, as luck would have it, an old bullet that he had found in a field. Hector said that it had never occurred to him that it was an actual bullet. He put it into the prop gun. I'm not sure he actually understood that it wasn't a real gun, and unfortunately, some models of prop gun sometimes work if they are loaded with a real bullet. It was a tragic set of unfortunate coincidences.'

'And his father didn't get the role?' Sylvia asked.

'No. Roger Grave, the director, didn't give it to him, because he knew he couldn't do it justice,' said Julia. 'We heard the audition, Tabitha and I. Hector is a really terrible actor.'

'Indescribably bad,' Tabitha concurred.

'So Troilus killed the director?'

'Yes,' Julia nodded. 'I don't think Troilus meant to kill him. He just wanted to persuade him that his father was right for the part. Wanted to *do* something for Hector. But things got out of hand.'

Hayley nodded. 'That's his story, and I believe it. He threw the Shakespeare book at Grave, and Grave fell and hit his head.'

Tabitha shook her head sadly. 'I just can't believe that two people are dead over a part in an amateur play!'

'It was nearly three people,' Sean said with a shudder. He reached over and took Julia's hand. 'He came to Julia's house. He threatened to...' He could hardly say the words.

'Oh, I don't think it would have come to that. I don't think he would really have harmed me,' said Julia, with more certainty than she felt. It had turned out that Troilus had an iron poker in his satchel, which Julia had a horrible feeling would have been a far more effective weapon than *The Complete Works of Shakespeare*. She reminded herself that it hadn't come to that. 'Anyway, Hayley showed up just in time, so all's well that ends well.'

Sylvia looked at Hayley, her eyes wide with admiration. 'You saved the day?' she asked.

'Thanks to Julia's quick thinking.' She turned to Julia. 'It's just as well you managed to get that message to me and let me know you were in need of help.'

'And it's just as well you got the message, understood what was going on, and came rushing to my rescue! The way you tackled Troilus to the floor when you got there – it was so brave and clever. I'll never forget the sight of you sitting on his back, holding him down.'

'I was just doing my job,' the detective inspector said modestly. There was a pause. 'I only wish I'd got to the answer earlier. If we'd worked out Graham Powell's murder earlier, Roger Grave would still be alive.'

'I don't think you could have suspected that a man would be killed over a role in an amateur play,' said Sylvia, absolutely decisively, and Hayley smiled at her.

'Food's on the table,' Jono called through the door. Indeed, the smell of melted cheese and oregano and hot olive oil wafted tantalisingly towards them. Julia felt her mouth water and her tummy rumble in anticipation.

'Come along, everyone,' she said, and led the way to the table.

'It's absolutely delicious,' said Tabitha, once they had all been served and were tucking in. 'I think it might be the best lasagne I've ever had. And I've had quite a few!' She patted her soft tummy, and laughed.

'It's my mum's special recipe. She taught me how to make it. She was sick... but she made sure I got the hang of it before she died. I wanted to make it to say thanks to Dad and Julia for all the good meals they've been making for me.'

Jono's touching story was met with a thoughtful silence, which he broke with a joke: 'And to impress Laine, of course.'

Everyone laughed. Laine blushed.

The lasagne was so good it was polished off, and the last crispy bits scraped off the sides with a spoon.

'Fantastic meal.' Sean reached over and put his hand on top of his son's. 'Your mum would be pleased to know you made her recipe for the people you care about. She'd be proud of you, Jono.'

'Would she?' he asked. There was a tiny tremor in his voice.

'Oh yes, without a doubt! Your resilience, your kindness, your gift with animals. And as for this lasagne... Your mum would be proud as punch.'

'She'd be proud of us both, Dad.' Jono glanced over at Julia and said, 'I know that she'd be happy to see you happy, Dad.'

'Ah, look at us, getting all sentimental.' Sean's tone managed to be both gruff and tender.

'Nothing wrong with a bit of sentimentality,' said Julia. 'Life is unpredictable. We must appreciate what we have.'

'Indeed we must. And we do.' He gave her a loving smile.

'And I happen to have chocolate brownies, which I made just this morning, and which I think people might appreciate right about now,' she said.

'I'm sure you're right on that score,' said Hayley.

'Well, if you clear the table, I'll fetch the brownies.'

A LETTER FROM KATIE GAYLE

Dear reader,

By now you might know that Katie Gayle is, in fact, two of us – Kate and Gail. As we publish Julia Bird's seventh adventure, and our tenth book as Katie Gayle, we look back at this journey that we have taken with Julia and have to pinch ourselves – it started with us just having fun and turned into a world that so many of you enjoy. We hope that you have loved this latest visit to Berrywick, and that you approve of the introduction of Chaplin into the Bird household!

We're hard at work on more adventures for Julia and Jake and the people of Berrywick. If you want to keep up to date with all Katie Gayle's latest releases, just sign up at the following link. Your email address will never be shared and you can unsubscribe at any time.

www.bookouture.com/katie-gayle

You can also follow us on Twitter and Facebook for regular updates and pictures of the real-life Jake! We really love hearing from you – especially those of you who have found Julia a help during difficult times in your life.

The best thing that you can do for us is to write a review and post it on Amazon and Goodreads, so that other people can discover Julia and Jake too. Ratings and reviews really help writers!

You might also enjoy our Epiphany Bloom series – the first three books are available for download now. We think that they are very funny.

You can find us in a few places and we'd love to hear from you.

Katie Gayle is on Twitter as @KatieGayleBooks and on Facebook as Katie Gayle Writer. On Twitter or X or whatever you want to call it, you can also follow Kate at @katesidley and Gail at @gailschimmel. Kate and Gail are also on Insta and Threads, and Gail, for her sins, is trying to figure out TikTok! Our website is katiegaylebooks.com.

Thanks,

Katie Gayle

facebook.com/KatieGayleWriter
x.com/KatieGayleBooks

PUBLISHING TEAM

Turning a manuscript into a book requires the efforts of many people. Katie Gayle and the publishing team at Bookouture would like to acknowledge everyone who contributed to this publication.

Audio
Alba Proko
Melissa Tran
Sinead O'Connor

Commercial
Lauren Morrissette
Hannah Richmond
Imogen Allport

Cover design
The Brewster Project

Data and analysis
Mark Alder
Mohamed Bussuri

Editorial
Nina Winters
Imogen Allport

Copyeditor
Gabbie Chant

Proofreader
Jenny Page

Marketing
Alex Crow
Melanie Price
Occy Carr
Cíara Rosney
Martyna Młynarska

Operations and distribution
Marina Valles
Stephanie Straub
Joe Morris

Production
Hannah Snetsinger
Mandy Kullar
Jen Shannon
Ria Clare

Publicity
Kim Nash
Noelle Holten
Jess Readett
Sarah Hardy

Rights and contracts
Peta Nightingale
Richard King
Saidah Graham